Shakespe~re'~ R~~~

By H~~~, ~~~~~

With deep acknowledgment to William Shakespeare
half a thousand years later this miracle has might that in black ink
his love shall still shine bright.

www.publishnation.co.uk

Cover image (1507-1510) by kind permission of the
The Morgan Library & Museum
225 Madison Avenue
New York, NY 10016-3405

CONTENTS: CHAPTER TITLES

Chapter One
The tale I was told

This is the story I was told by my dear friend Hamnet Shakespeare, about how I, Mummer the Bear, came to live with the Shakespeare family in Stratford on Avon. I had been found, near death, at dawn one day in the Forest of Arden. I was discovered by the children of a pedlar who was passing through the forest. He had stopped his wagon in a clearing on the road to Stratford, so that his horses could rest in the shade. The children had climbed down off the wagon to play, and were running and laughing while chasing each other deeper into the forest.

Fickle chance sometimes sends happy gifts! I might have perished if those children had not found me. At first they thought my mother had abandoned me after I was born, without even licking her poor little helpless cub and coaxing the life into my tiny body. But then the pedlar had heard news about a bear that had been killed nearby by woodsmen. That must have been my mother, so I was lucky to have escaped and to have been found by the children who saved me. Each night the pedlar, helped by the children, set next to the wagon some hempen twines and wooden posts from which they draped the sheepskins they planned to sell. In the daytime they would travel to attend the markets in the nearby midland towns where they sold weaves. When they found me they put me in a basket of straw – an unlicked cub not much thought upon, washed now by the pedlar's children and wrapped again in some coarse cloth. I mewled and cried with hunger and they fed me with milk. I lived with the pedlar's family for a month, resting in a child's arms at the back of the wagon, as we sped along the dusty pathways through the autumn forest, with its bracken and birch, hearing strange howls in the dark nights, when the moon sometimes shone. My legs grew longer, my paws grew and spread wider. I opened my eyes after that first month and that which I had smelt and tasted became whole to me in sight and sound. The taste of the milk in the pouch made from a pig's bladder, and the feel of crushed berries in my mouth, all became alive to me. In the firelight the wandering pedlars sang their songs of another land, in eerie haunting melodies.

Soon that autumn, when the yellow leaves were upon the ground, the pedlar told his children that I had grown too big for them to keep. I would grow yet bigger and must, perforce, be sold, in the marketplace.

Hamnet told me my story some years later. It was one night while we were upon our great journey to London. After feeding me he sat with me, the door to my cage open and we rested in the moonlight in the yard of Lord Makepeace's house in the midst of the Forest, because we were lodging there that night. I nuzzled up to the boy in the soft forest night, the flares of the yard lamps at Lord Makepeace's great house flickering behind us. Hamnet said to me:

"My dear Mummer, I will tell thee how we met. Upon my fifth birthday, nigh on three years ago, my Father, William Shakespeare, came into my small chamber and gave me a small golden coin. That day he spake to me and told me I would always have gold. 'What may I do with it father?' I asked him.

'You should keep it about you and never lose it. One day you may see something where naught else will do but you must have it. Why then, you may purchase your dream with this golden disc.'

For two years I kept it upon a leather cord around my neck. Then came the day of my seventh Birthday, in February 1592, when I first met you, Mummer. My father William came into my room to wish me a fine and joyous day.

'Come, Hamnet my boy! We must forthwith wake thy sister Judith for she is thy twin and born this very day, moments after thee. And today the both of you are seven years of age!'

'But my sister Judith is a longer sleeper and we shall surprise her,' I said, but then we heard a noise outside the room.

'Methinks we shall not surprise her,' said my father. 'She and your elder sister Susanna and Mistress Anne, thy good mother are already here. So here upon their cue they arrived.

Then did the family Shakespeare walk together into the centre of town of Stratford upon Avon. That day was a market day. Judith and Susanna went with Mistress Anne to the Haberdasher, and my Father and I walked among the stalls. Master William was greeted by many of the folk we passed, for he was a renowned Stratford man. And whilst he was stopped in conversation with a neighbour, I slipped

2

away and wandered down a narrow lane in the market and came upon a pedlar's wagon ...'"

And so it was that very day, in Stratford-upon-Avon market, his ears being keen, Hamnet had discovered me crying and mewling among the pots and weaves and straw, still wrapped in my coarse dirty hempen sack upon the pedlar's wagon. He haggled with the pedlar, who confirmed that indeed I was a bear cub, freshly left in the forest abandoned by my birth mother bear, that very month, and brought hither by the pedlar's own children. And thus Hamnet bought me, giving in exchange his most precious possession: that small Turkish gold coin with a hole in the middle, that, years before, his father William had put upon a leather plait and with his own hands placed tenderly around Hamnet's neck. Upon cradling me in his arms and lifting me gently off the wagon, Hamnet held me close as he walked through the streets and fields of Stratford upon Avon to his home.

In the kitchen of the cottage, Hamnet fed me from a leather bottle. His mother Anne had been most kind and boiled up some goat's milk and water and given it to him for me. After the milk had cooled Hamnet gave me the bottle's leather teat to suck. This must have brought a feeling of warmth and sunshine into my mind, now being such a loved and well-fed cub. Of course I could now smell new scents and hear the voices of humans and see them. Hamnet told me that tears came from my eyes.

His father William entered the kitchen and came to peer at me, before he stood, as I now know he does, legs apart in front of the fire by the hearth where I was being fed and filled with goats' milk and love – and sunshine, which I could feel and now could see.

Chapter Two
My Life in Stratford

I am recalling all this now that I am an old bear and thus, no longer in my best years, live now at the pleasure of fair or whimsical chance. I have lived through many adventures and alarums and times of desperate dangers and sweet delights and more yet, in this powerful but fragile land of England. This Tudor realm was most dangerous for bears then and in many centuries past! In this realm I loved and I was loved by the Shakespeare family: Master Hamnet Shakespeare, the finder and founder of my feast of life, and his sisters Susanna and Judith, and Mistress Anne Shakespeare the ruler of the Shakespeare household and all that pertained thereto, and her husband the Poet, Great Observer of life and Playwright, Master William Shakespeare. Here I learned to understand the words they spoke and remember them well and yet more. So I knew the sense thereof when they spoke of Caesars and Kings and Queens and mighty dukes, yet when I tried to speak them out, came there only a growl. As Hamnet carried on the story, I began to remember what happened when I came into the Shakespeare house.

"What's this, Hamnet?" Shakespeare had boomed, "Another puppy? Have we not enough stray dogs about the place?' He peered at me, "Still matted – a strange looking dog at that!"

Judith, Hamnet's sister, piped up. "It looks sick and like to die."

The whole family looked at me.

"If it lives, may I keep it, father?" asked Hamnet.

William Shakespeare filled a pewter tankard with ale from a small cask and watched his son. "If it lives, you may keep him, Hamnet, though we already have enough hounds to be sure!"

Judith laughed as did they all,

"But Father dear, a hound is this none," said Hamnet.

"Nay father," said Judith, "can you not tell what creature this is that Hamnet hath given his golden ducat for?"

" He gave his golden piece forsooth! What name doth he have, this strange little dog, your new pet?"

"Thank you father," said Hamnet. "I have not named him yet."

Judith gave a peal of laughter. "But it is not a hound, Father. It is a bear cub!"

Master Shakespeare bent down to look at me closer. He bore the scent of wonderful fruits and flowers. "Why so it is! An unlicked bear whelp abandoned by its dam, methinks, who hath known no impression of her."

He seemed to bring kindness and love to me, and tickled me

"He is to be an actor, father."

"Yet he cannot speak his lines," said Master Shakespeare.

"Why then we must name him Mummer," said Hamnet.

"Why so?" asked Judith.

"A Mummer is an actor, a fine and skilled entertainer, who speaks not but doth mime his part," replied Hamnet.

"Actor or no, his cub's life is but a summer's lease," said Master Shakespeare. "Soon he will grow into a mighty bear, a wild creature, and then shalt thou not know him like today, for then I be afeard that thou wilt find his savageness. As sweet as he suckles with thee now, there will come a dark day when thou may not know him with his bear's wild temper, nor satisfy thyself as to what thou may do with him."

"But he will not be wild, father," cried Hamnet. "I promise you, I shall raise and train him, school him like unto a fine hound, and he shall be good and sweet unto all, for he will know no wildness or danger. I shall love his savagery away from him and give him no cause to be angry nor afraid of me."

"Of you or any humans, I hope," said Master William.

For some reason I growled and they all laughed.

And so it was in the year 1592 I joined the household of Mr William Shakespeare.

Chapter Three
Master Shakespeare pens his plays

Master William Shakespeare was a handsome man. He was at all times richly dressed in velvet and white linen, and had a fine domed head and crisp beard and a wise yet jolly look. In his hand he often held a parchment from which he studied and then read aloud to Hamnet and myself. He smelt of leather and lavender.

Oft as a small cub would I play about them whilst Master Shakespeare wrote upon his parchment, his fine feather quill darting across the page and scrawling these mysterious symbols which became, as I observed him and heard him speak, words in his mouth. Sometimes he spoke them aloud to Hamnet, who tickled and teased me. Master Shakespeare would laugh uproariously – Hamnet and he made much merriment together as I growled and licked their faces. I would play upon Hamnet's knee, supping at a leather bottle some milk that Mistress Anne had warmed for me.

Thus began my love for Hamnet, who fed and cuddled me and spoke to me softly that I was a good cub. He would hold me tight unto him and call me "Mummer bear" and "Mummer boy" and used to pet me and snuggle me. Somehow I seemed to have in my bear's mind some device for understanding what they spoke about me.

"That cub is a long sleeper and drinks much sheep's milk," said Judith. "Maybe he will have the temper of a sheep!" She laughed.

"But he is not a hound, my child," said her father. "Why, since ancient times hounds and dogs have been the companions of men, have hunted with them and guarded them, but there is no such history with the bear. Quite otherwise! You cannot take the savagery out of the wild beast."

"But what of St. Francis and the Wolf, father?" quoth Hamnet. "How he tamed Brother Wolf and exhorted the people that they should feed the creature?"

William Shakespeare laughed and slapped his thigh. "Oh my fine boy! Art thou St Francis come anew?"

" Just because there is no story, father, it means not that a thing cannot be accomplished," said Hamnet.

This of course happened long before I ran up a tree in fright and would not come down for a day until I became hungry, though Hamnet and Judith did entice me with sweetmeats and berries and potage. But most days of my early life at Stratford they would feed me many times with goat's milk and honey from a leather suckling bag.

When I was a small cub I slept next to Hamnet. As I grew bigger I slept in a basket by Hamnet's bed and then later by the hearth in the kitchen, although the smells of food drove me a little crazy. One night I somewhat wrenched asunder and pulled off the larder door. Climbing over its fallen broken pieces I entered therein and found nuts, honey, berries, apples and some sweet tasting liquid which made me very happy. I supped upon them all very well in a mighty feast, then fell asleep among the ruins, wherein I was found in the morning by Mistress Anne and her house servant Joan wielding a broom.

Hamnet saved me from a thrashing, holding his arm aloft to shield me from the broom. "He won't do it again mother ..."

"That bear will eat us out of house and home" said Mistress Anne crossly, looking at the mess.

Hamnet spoke up. "I will teach him. It wasn't fair to leave him in the kitchen. Bears have greater noses than do we and finer even than hounds. They can smell a hundred dozen times better than we can," he said.

"Then thou must show all the world, my boy, that thou can tame the wild beast." His mother replied.

Mistress Anne could not abide me near the hearth of their resting chamber, and she chased me away with a broom from there, often shouting to Hamnet that I would bring with me insects and creeping petty things into their clean bed.

After that they put a stouter door upon the larder and I was banished from the house. From dawn all day I dwelt within the garden wherein Hamnet and Judith had made a wooden hutch for me. I was fed on titbits from the kitchen, and berries. I soon outgrew the hutch and at night was put to sleep at the rear of the cottage, at the step of the kitchen, in a large basket. I was but a small cub then learning my way around life in the Shakespeare's household. Mr Shakespeare soon had a young carpenter build for me a bearcub's den, a small but veritable house by the kitchen garden. I was placed therein at nights with straw for bedding, and my bowl for feed was put at the entranceway. The hounds and geese and pigs were not so well treated nor accommodated.

Hamnet would appear each morning long after the sun had risen, but Judith was up earlier and would feed me first before she fed the Shakespeares' geese and chickens who swiftly made a great noise when she approached.

My early cub seasons were wonderful, filled with love from Hamnet, Judith, Anne and William and indeed all the Shakespeare family. But all too soon they passed. The hounds were a nuisance but after one bit my ear and I bit the hound back we all seemed to get along. I was much favoured and I think the dogs were jealous. I was allowed to roll and run and play in the garden, where I chased butterflies and was tickled on the tummy by Hamnet and his sister.

I was often peckish, and in the mornings I would eat oaten broth, which Hamnet would make and feed me with at the back door. We would romp out into the fields behind the cottage. Hamnet would run and I would chase after him. I loved the scent of the meadows. Endlessly I would tug at branches and sniff my way through the undergrowth, swiping at butterflies with my paws, resting after a long chase and drinking water from a small spring whilst Hamnet cradled me. And afterwards I would lie in the meadow in the sunlight whilst Judith sang a sweet song and Hamnet fed me berries.

One day Hamnet stood at the door of his father's study. "Must I go to school Papa?" he asked. "I would sooner stay here with you."

"Alas my dear child, thy scholarly knowledge is the fountain at which thou must drink – thy cornucopia. You must learn of language, of nations, of princes, of history, and of Latin!"

Hamnet kicked the door as he left, and Mr Shakespeare and I watched as he slowly walked away.

Mr Shakespeare said to me:
"The whining schoolboy, with his satchel,
And shining morning face, creeping like a snail
Unwillingly to school."
And his pen flew across his parchment.

Sometimes when Hamnet was at school I would sleep in my basket by Mr Shakespeare's feet as he wrote at his great dark desk. When I was awake he fed me with pieces of apple and cheese which remained from his own meal and all day in the summer we had strawberries from the garden.

He spoke and he wrote. I stood with my paws upon his knee as Mr Shakespeare dipped his mighty feather pen into a silver inkwell. As he wrote he paused and looked down at me and spoke:

"Wherefore go thou forth into Venice …" He stared for while up at the oak beams in the ceiling and gazed down at me again. I nodded. He turned to his manuscript and then he wrote something down. He looked at me again, saying "and see there what my credit may do," and popped a piece of apple in my mouth.

Thus began my very first summer's lease as a cub with the Shakespeare family in Stratford-upon-Avon. Soon I was no longer a helpless cub but a curious creature keen to discover the world beyond the Shakespeare family hearth.

Hamnet would take me out to play in the fields around and near their home. When we came to the field he would unleash the lead from my collar and let me run free and would chase me, while Judith's puppy would run with us. I would roll and wrestle with the little dog. Now that I had grown a little, Hamnet and Judith would take me for walks into the woodland forests which became my playground.

"He is not a beast nor monster," said Hamnet. "He is a sweet gentle creature and knows only love from us."

My passion was to wrestle and tumble with Hamnet and to kiss and lick his face. I also ate joyously in the forest. The smells and scents of the leaves and fruits overwhelmed me. Hamnet and Judith would lead the way and I would romp behind them, exploring bushes and trees whose fruitful branches had flourished many a year. The boughs and brambles were a constant delight to me, as were new smells, and flying creatures like birds, insects and butterflies. This was my first spring.

Once I bit Hamnet's hand without knowing or realizing the sharpness of my little teeth and received a stern rebuke before he pushed me into a stream. I climbed out much chastened. Later upon our walk I saw stripy baby creatures. "Badgers," said Hamnet, holding down a branch with small fruits near to me that I might eat them, as the stripy creatures scampered away, I was sorry that they had run away as they were furry and I thought they would be good playmates, but Hamnet drew me away, fearing their mother's bite.

9

The woodland with its briars provided a wonderful new world of roots, and berries upon the sprig. Sometimes I pushed my nose into sharp thorns.

But we were not always in the forest. One day I recall Master Shakespeare was playing and writing and speaking as if he were a great King. "Come hither my boy."

Hamnet moved toward him dutifully, silent, with his eyes lowered. His father wrote and said,

"Let me kiss my boy." Then the playwright leaned forward and kissed Hamnet's cheek. Mr Shakespeare explained to his audience, Hamnet and myself, thus: "This is the day of the King's recoronation."

"What is a recoronation, Father?" asked Hamnet.

"Why, when the King says, 'Once more we sit upon England's royal throne, repurchased with the blood of enemies,' he is referring to having lost the crown in earlier times and now having fought battles and killed those who would have the throne. Then he takes the throne again for himself and is re-crowned. Now he addresses his son before the court," said his father.

He went on writing and speaking, while I suckled upon the teat of the bottle of goat's milk. He spoke in a booming voice: *"Young man, for thee ... Thine uncles and I watched in our armour all the winter's night, went all afoot in summer's scalding heat, that thou might be possessed the crown in peace."*

Mr Shakespeare paused, and peered at the parchment, wrote, and then spoke once more, " From our labours thou shall reap the gain."

"Yes, I like that," he muttered. Then he spoke to us once more. The King says, *"Sweet babe"* and invites his brothers, both powerful Dukes, to kiss the Prince.

"Why, father?" asked Hamnet.

"Why, thus to show their loyalty and allegiance to him, the King, and also to his son so that he should reign next." And his brother the Duke says, *"As I love the tree from whence thou sprangst ..."*

Chapter Four
I learn about London and the
'Sport' of Bear-Baiting

As I grew bigger, Mistress Anne Shakespeare became anxious. One day she cried: "Hamnet, that bear shall eat our fortune! It will much disable our own estate. See as he approaches – he grows so big he can scarce come into the kitchen without he fills the room. He cannot stay like this. These butchers' bills will stretch even thy father's stout purse."

"Oh Father, good Father," cried Hamnet, "what are we to do?"

"He must be put to earning money!" Mistress Anne crossed her arms and looked stern. Master Shakespeare nodded sagely, but Hamnet cried, "Oh Father, you will not bait him nor see him chained at the stake to be savaged by beastly feral hounds!"

And Judith said, "He is such a sweet and gentle bear that he knows not of an angry mood nor bares he his tusks at any of us."

"He has not tusks!" laughed Hamnet.

I looked at my paws, which were indeed grown large and long, and I knew my teeth were sharp. Master Shakespeare, whose love still shone bright in good black ink, looked upon me kindly and I felt his love toward me. He patted my furry head and I nuzzled his hand. He reassured them: "Nay, children, they shall not bait him! He is too young, too gentle, too childish-foolish for this cruel world and should not meet hearts of men who seek beasts to draw blood for their sport. Mummer is not made nor mannered for such sportive tricks, such bloody games!" He played with his quill and chewed the feather upon its end, as he continued to think aloud. "Methinks that as he plays so well with a ball and walks so gracefully with his paw out, sporting a cloth draped about him like a Caesar, perchance we should put him upon the stage in London."

"As the distinguished actor bear!" cried Judith.

"If he is to be an actor then forthwith , Hamnet ye must teach him skills," said Master Shakespeare.

11

"But father, I know nothing of teaching a bear to act!"

"Indeed" said Master Shakespeare, "what learned scholar is there who knows such a thing as the teaching of acting unto an animal?"

Shakespeare paused as the door burst open and, very flustered, Mistress Anne just then did appear.

"My husband, there is here one from London, who says he is Master Philip Henslowe ..."

    * * **

Now I am an old Bear and have learned much, but then I was yet to discover that in this Elizabethan age, whilst the Queen ruled the Country, beneath her one man ruled supreme over a vast and cruel world which encompassed the fearsome sport of Bear Baiting, where poor innocent bears were captured from the forests and forced to fight against snapping snarling savage hounds, for the sport and amusement of the people. That man was Philip Henslowe, the Master of the Queen's Bears and Grand Purveyor of shows both fierce and brutal. These contests of gore were held in great theatres wherein the crowds would shout and drink and place bets upon their chosen bear, or against the bear, placing their wager upon the hounds. There were famous bears called names like Harry Hunks, George Stone ,Tom of Lincoln, Blind Ned, and Sackerson. The populace made heroes of these great bears, while their cunning owners were usually in partnership with this Mr Henslowe. He built the bear-gardens, bear-pits and theatres, managed their shows, and reigned like the Devil himself over these pits of sorrow, cruelty, pain and death. This much I came to know, and the first time I heard of this damned underworld was that night, from the conversation of Mr. Shakespeare and his family.

"They say Mr Henslowe is one of the richest men in England and owns many taverns, some of ill repute, and many bawdy houses," said Suzanne, looking up from her embroidery.

"And Mr Henslowe hath a treasure of gold in leather pouches and silver too," said Mistress Anne. "he gleaneth it from his frightful wicked bear pits at Paris Gardens. Much treasure. "It is hid so that thieves should not rob him."

"Why yes," said Mr. Shakespeare. " 'Tis said he keeps it under the cage of the fiercest bears!"

Hamnet and Judith looked alarmed.

12

"He is not here for Mummer, Father? You promised he would not be baited."

"Fear not, my children, Mr. Henslowe is here to see me on business, and he is awaiting my joining him forthwith in our parlour." Master William stood up.

"What business?" asked Mistress Anne shrewdly.

"Why, he is rebuilding a theatre called the Rose in London, and wants that my Company and the Chamberlain's men do stage shows there. You, Hamnet, have a bear that wants work. Perhaps he shall guard my coin! For thy bear shall go to London with us. Taking the bear is a great expense but yet we can encompass it."

Master Shakespeare said to his wife, "Henslowe makes much money. He is richer in income and land than many a duke, and makes sure that the Queen is apprised of which bear to wager upon and when the bear shall prevail over the hounds."

"But how would he know that, father?" asked Judith.

"Why not all is as it seems. Cunning men do create sportive shows upon which the public may wager, yet the outcome is assured by complots – secret favouring of certain bears that become renowned and famous for their alleged victories. Such bears like *Harry Hunks* and *Sackerson* become well known to the general populace. These evil shows with their fireworks and mummers, jesters and spectacles of blood and bone, are the money engines which fill the coffers of Henslowe with golden ducats, and which enable him to rebuild a theatre, the Rose, which is now to be dedicated for the acting of plays by Mr William Shakespeare and his Chamberlain's Company of Actors."

"And, I pray, the making of our family fortunes" said Mistress Anne.

                              * ***

Mr Henslowe was full of gratitude for his supper. "I do thank you for your kind welcomes and amply thank thee Mistress for the fine meal and good Warwickshire hospitality of the Shakespeare hearth!" said the builder of the Rose Theatre, Master of the Queen's Bears and *impresario* of the dreaded bear pits of Paris Gardens.

"Why, thank thee, Mr. Henslowe, thou art most welcome."

Philip Henslowe peered round and his eye caught Hamnet and me. "And is this thy son Hamnet?" he asked.

13

"Aye, he is nine years and we think already unto his education."

"And young Hamnet, what creature is this, sirrah?"

I cowered behind Hamnet for I had just heard about this man, this monster!

"Why, 'tis a bear cub, Master Henslowe," said Hamnet.

"He seems afeared to be a bear," laughed Henslowe, and William politely joined in the laugh as they supped at their ale.

"He is but a young cub, sir and knows not the wild and fighting ways of bears," said Hamnet.

Henslowe reached forward and pulled hard at my chin. I growled.

"Oh but the fierceness is within him for sure."

Now this age was ruled over by Her Great Majesty Queen Elizabeth the first, the Queen of England, a mighty lady much loved by the most of her subjects but much feared and hated by others. This royal person, this fount of sunlight and wisdom, this great warrior defender of England and patron of sciences, was sadly also an enthusiast for the dreadful ill-named "Sport" of the baiting of bears, which means fighting them sometimes to their deaths against savage hounds for the entertainment of the masses, and was now much carried on in London and other places, whence crowds would come and pay admission to the shows, which would

forerun the theatre as a mass entertainment.

I feared that soon would come a time when Master Shakespeare and his son Hamnet would perforce have me reside and fight in the terrible cages of the bear-pits whether they willed it or no.

Master Shakespeare looked kindly upon his son. "It is a good thing thy father is grown so rich and with such movables that we need not talk thereof."

"Yes," said Mistress Anne, "for in his theatres your kind father doth stage such plays that the groundlings and merchants and nobles will come and will pay much coin in copper, silver and gold to see and hear them. Shakespeare's Players Company actors add colour to the chameleon, change place with Proteus for advantages and put the murderous Machiavel to school."

"My own dear wife, my very words! Now shall we take Mummer to London? He can learn to act upon the stage, and will preserve our coin under his cage."

14

"When do we travel there?" asked Hamnet. "For I fear for him at the bear baiting places."

"Why father, that bear is too childish-foolish for the wild wilderness," said Judith. "He would not long thrive as he hath lost his hunting soul and doth wish no more than to be friends with every creature. Why, he was frightened by a furry centipede and jumped back from it … Can we tell what is in the heart of a wild beast?" Judith asked her father.

She looked at me and I licked her face.

"Aye we know each other's faces, but for our hearts, he knows no more of mine, than I of yours; nor I no more of his, than you of mine," she mused.

****

I was growing fast. My legs seemed to have shot out to a great length and my paws increased. Methought I was a child of the Shakespeare family but with more fur. Hamnet fed me mornings with milk and beaten eggs cooked in a pot, and bread and fruits from his father's writing room, and a supper of broth and porridge in the evening, at the back door of the cottage.

We were to travel unto London after Easter, when the winter had passed and golden spring blossomed in the garden of Mistress Anne Shakespeare and in the fields and meadows around. I, Mummer, now had a collar with a medallion which said, "This Bear is the true property of Hamnet Shakespeare of Stratford upon Avon." I now proudly bore this collar and Hamnet said, "There, thou shalt never be lost to us for we love thee, little bear."

Chapter Five
Master Banks and His Horse Morocco

Everyone in the household was excited. We were due to have a visit in Stratford from the renowned Mr. Banks with his horse Morocco. They were known all over Europe for their acting and tricks and they were now touring England. Master Shakespeare had invited them to visit us when they were in Stratford, and Mr. Greenaway, a neighbour, had just brought Mr Banks' reply that he would be honoured and delighted to do so.

Master Shakespeare told Hamnet, "He stays for a month. Use that time well, my son. Observe him and his famous Horse Morocco! I will entreat him to share with thee the magical art of training an animal for the theatre."

Sensing this was all about me, I growled loudly and happily, and everyone laughed. Hamnet said, "I can see the billboards now! Mummer the Renowned Actor Bear appearing at the Rose theatre, with his skillful trainer Master Hamnet Shakespeare." I thus was stepping out towards my stage career.

As the day approached, there was an air of expectation in the household – things were afoot! Hamnet had given me a special wash and then Judith had petted me, and gently plaited my fur with coloured silk ribbons.

There was not room enough for Mr. Banks and his entourage of some three men with horses to stay in our home so they were all accommodated at the White Swan Inn. The mirthful comic show was to be staged in the field next to the courtyard of the Inn. As we made our way into the town in the late afternoon, we were stared at by knots of people moving in the same direction. We caused a ripple and the people moved all apart from us as we walked. Except for the children – for soon we were accompanied by a chattering chittering forest of young girls and boys. "Good sir, what's the bear's name?" cried one.

16

"Mummer," Hamnet replied. This excited the squealing, squeaking, happy children, and they kept repeating my name: "Ooh look, Ooh look, there is yon Mummer, a bear." Mummer, Mummer! My name passed many times between them and it thrilled me to hear it. When we arrived at the field abutting the courtyard of the White Swan Inn of Stratford, there was a great crowd, many of them standing around supping tankards of ale as they gossiped, and families sitting on the grass eating.

We stopped, surrounded by curious children reaching out shyly to touch me. I nibbled berries from Hamnet's hand as he read a notice pinned upon a great tree:

ONE NIGHT ONLY!

See the Great Show of Mr. Banks and his Wondrous Horse Morocco. Fresh from their Triumphs in Paris, the capital of France, to our own English land. They took by storm the town of Shrewsbury and the city of Oxford!

Mr. Banks will cause Morocco to perform strange and magical tricks the like of which hath ne'er been seen! Prices sixpence for the Royal stand, three pence the courtyard and a penny the groundlings and upon the wall!

Morocco is the world's wisest animal. For another penny he will answer questions.

At the gate Hamnet paid six pence to join the exclusive audience in the front courtyard. "No charge for the bear!" said the gatekeeper with a laugh, while the crowd swirled around us putting coins in his hand. Soon the press of people became strong and the lamps flared brighter as dusk gathered. The crowd was good natured and happy.

In the courtyard we watched the firework displays from the walled garden and endured the shrieks of the crowd as the Minstrels worked among them. The lamps were beginning to be lit even though it was yet not dusk and there were firework displays and jesters as well as tents and carts selling sweetmeats and roasted meat near to the Inn. We joined Master Shakespeare and the family, all in fine clothing and at the very front of the audience. Judith patted and hugged me. Taking the berry basket from Hamnet she fed me from her hand. Then came a special moment. The Innkeeper called for quiet and announced, "My Lords, ladies and Gentlemen, the White Swan Inn is proud to present,

17

straight from their tour of the Continent and the Shires, the celebrated theatrical act and comic show, Banks and Morocco."

There was a great cheer from the crowd and into the courtyard from the Inn side came a stylish man, finely and fashionably dressed in brown silk with white knee britches and a large feathered hat. Trotting beside him was a pure white horse, with plaits and bells in his mane, very bright and alert looking.

"His hooves are shod in silver," whispered Master Shakespeare.

Banks commanded the horse: "Morocco, take a bow." The horse stepped forward, lowered his head and bent his front legs in a graceful gesture, with his head nearly touching the ground. The audience applauded and whistled.

"Mummer, what say you to that?" asked Hamnet. I had never before been so excited, with the fireworks, the crowd of people all cheering and the beautiful horse Morocco doing what his lord bade him to do.

"Now count to four!" cried Mr Banks. Morocco lifted up his hoof for a moment and then struck it upon the cobblestones once, twice, thrice and then four times. Renewed applause from the crowd.

"Master Shakespeare, lend me your purse," cried Banks. He looked inside and then rattled the purse in Morocco's ear. "How many coins?" he demanded. The horse tapped six times, and Mr Banks patted the horse and roared out "Right". He handed it back to Mr Shakespeare who confirmed that indeed he had six coins in the purse.

Banks again addressed the horse, "Now find me the veriest richest rogue in Stratford!" Morocco moved around the ring and then nuzzled the shoulder of the Innkeeper, John Low. The audience roared and the Innkeeper laughed at the jest.

"Mummer, I could teach you these tricks," whispered Hamnet. "I perceive that whilst all are watching the horse, Banks is giving clucking signals with his mouth, or snapping his fingers."

Then Banks ordered Morocco to lie down and play dead, which he did right dutifully. "Rise up," he then commanded and the horse rose and jogged and trotted most daintily.

"Morocco, bow for the Queen!" called Banks. The white horse once more gracefully lowered his head and forelegs. "Now stoop for the King of Spain," he called, whereupon the horse reared up and whinnied, began to chomp with his teeth, pawed the ground with his hoof angrily and shook his head.

Then Banks called him to seek out a man in the assembled company whose coat sported a red silk lining to his coat, and a lady wearing a green shawl. Both of these did he move unerringly towards.

Morocco would "deliver" upon command, accepting in his mouth a glove or cloth from Banks and take it to the person Banks had named: the man with the velvet cloak, or the lady with the braids.

Hamnet said to his father, "I venture that he puts a word in his speech which is a command for the horse, but how he taught the horse this I cannot fathom."

His father answered, "He comes to see us tomorrow. He stays here for a week, and I have engaged him, through coin and friendship, to teach you how to train your bear."

Hamnet could scarcely contain his excitement. His father simply whispered, "Learn well from Mr. Banks and then work hard."

The show continued. Morocco's eyes were covered with a cloak and three people in the audience were asked each to furnish a gold or silver coin and place it in a glove. When Banks removed the blindfold he bade Morocco tell how many coins were in the glove. The horse stamped three times. Then Banks asked him how many were gold and Morocco stamped once. The coins were then held up for the audience to see that this was true, and they roared their approval.

"Oh father," cried Hamnet, "This is like unto sorcery!"

"Others have said the same," said his father, "but perchance you and Mummer will do as marvelously."

* ** *

How that spring and summer flew by! In the field behind the Shakespeare's summer cottage, leased whilst the small and crowded old family home in Stratford was being refurbished, and whilst Mr. Shakespeare did dream and write, Hamnet and I were alike into a strange dream. We had as our tutors the renowned players, Mr. Banks and his magical horse Morocco. Morocco rested much in the field and was well tended and rubbed down by grooms, fed and watered and brushed, treated by humans unlike any animal that I had ever seen. He was guarded day and night by Mr. Greenaway's sons who slept in a tent near the field's gate. Often Mr. Banks and Mr. Shakespeare, enthroned upon two velvet chairs brought upon the grass, did sup from

19

tankards of wine and observe whilst Hamnet, trained by Mr Banks, taught me to lie down, to play dead, to bow, to roar upon command, to hold up my paws in two fists and growl. How I loved these tricks and the learning thereof! I was fed titbits and berries and small oaten sweetcakes with fruit in them.

Then there were the counting tricks. "That's it, Hamnet," cried Mr. Banks, "You cluck once for one, twice for two, and thrice for three." He made a noise like a quiet chicken, but Morocco lifted his head up and looked at us all. "But the clucking must of necessity be made close between you and the bear," said Banks, "and he shall hold his paw up as if lazily for 'once'; he must beat the ground once with each paw for 'twice', then must the bear stamp his foot three times upon the board for 'thrice'."

And thus I learned to count. And many sweetmeats and berries and cherries did I gain.

Hamnet under Mr. Banks' instructions gave small cries like mewls as he thus bade me. Thus I learned the clucks, puckers and mewls for the different coloured coins – silver, gold and copper – that Hamnet wished me to know. Hamnet would hold up a gold coin behind me and bid me look away, which I did, sometimes pretending to have a sly look round, which brought gales of laughter from Mr. Banks and Mr. Shakespeare and the family who were all watching now. Then he would hide three coins, each one under a bright cloth. He would invite me to find the gold and I would turn round and amble over to the small wooden board upon which the coins now lay under their cloths. I would lower my head near the cloths and pretend to smell and as I moved over to the next cloth did Hamnet give me the chicken cluck sound. When I heard it I would pull the cloth back with my teeth, revealing the coin. Hamnet would give my head a sweet rub and pop some succulent treat into my mouth. I became very good at all my tricks and signals, for this was the language of Hamnet and food!

I learned to cover my eyes with my paws and hold my paws behind my ears for listening, and to waggle my ears with my paws if Hamnet said "Lend me your ears."

Then I learned the art of playing dead. Bowing and strutting with a toga, and tangling myself in it, did I play Caesar whilst Hamnet read aloud of Caesar's death. And he taught me to bow and roar upon his command: " Mummer," he would cry "Bow before Her Majesty the

20

Queen!" I learned that those words meant a deep and graceful bow and then I must stand upright and roar. But when the words "Now bow for the King of Spain!" were spoken did I learn to take it as an insult, turning my back and waggling my bottom at the words and turning my head round and growling. How I enjoyed these games! I earned many berries and spoons of honey for these and other tricks. Thus did I learn both the arts theatrical of a true Mummer and the arts mirthful of a true Jester. Hamnet and I did learn the art of comic bear shows. We were ready to go to London.

* * * *

Those were very pleasant days. Hamnet would walk me into Stratford in a very proper mode. I wore a chain but it was as light as you could wish, and no mask. The people would stare but mostly were kind and loved me. They would say, "What a sweet young cub thou hast there Master Hamnet, and how pleasant he is." They would tender carrots and apples to Hamnet to feed me with, but he bade them feed me themselves. Thus I had the fortunate and pleasurable habit of being fed by human hand with succulent berries and sweetmeats into my soft bear mouth.

And one day in 1594 I heard Hamnet cry out, "Mummer! Judith!" He came to sit with us upon the grass knoll by the oak tree in the field at the back of the house. He hugged us both excitedly. "We are not to travel to London yet! The plague has closed the theatres and we are to rest here in Stratford for the good of our health!"

Thus it was that I came that spring to have more time loose in the garden, when my next great adventure happened ...

Chapter Six
In the Forest

It was in my second summer that I got into great trouble. One evening, in the garden, I met these large white creatures that were my biggest problem. Geese they are called. They terrified me when they squawked, and they chased me away from their goslings, thinking that I would eat their babies! As a flock they chased me, hissing and honking, flapping their wings and opening their great beaks. I scampered away from the mowed part wherein I had played with Hamnet and Judith many a time   and oft. I rushed on, my little bear's head full of noise, as the geese flapped and screamed behind me. Through the meadow and into the wood, still running and stumbling, I followed a butterfly into the forest.

The forest grew darker as the trees and brambles grew thicker. I scrambled on, still thinking that I heard those awful geese behind me, but the brambles scratched at me and eventually I stopped. There was moonlight in a small clearing in the forest. I smelt wildflowers and carrots. A huge smell and the sense of munching succulent juicy carrots came into my head. I was very hungry.

At the edge of the glade there was a small old roadway along which carts carried vegetables and livestock from the farms through the forest on to the Warwick road. Livestock such as pigs! I knew pigs from Mistress Anne's small pigsty at the end of the garden. They were noisy things and after a while I sometimes understood their grunts and they mine. I was usually fed after the pigs, as Mistress Anne was wont to say to Hamnet: "This bear eats thrice three times a day, my son." And he would reply, "And will eat us out of house and home!" They laughed as they spoke the words in chorus.

I wished I was back at the cottage now instead of in this fearful lonely place. An owl hooted. Now I was very hungry. The smell of a meal of carrots grew stronger. There at the far edge of the clearing, in the moonlight, was the source of the smell. A light mist wafted like a golden cloud toward my nose. I could almost *see* the smell shimmering in the darkness. A farmer's cart must have spilled a sack of carrots and the sack had burst open in the road.

Suddenly a strange lop-eared creature, not unlike Miss Judith's rabbit but much darker, hopped past me clutching a carrot between its teeth. Then it was gone. I could smell pig again but also a stranger darker stronger smell. And I could make out in the poor light two huge figures hunched over the carrots, munching. A few rabbits darted in and out at the edge of the carrot pile and occasionally one of the munching giant creatures growled and turned and stamped its strange shaped foot out at the daring rabbit. A thrilling frightening magical sparkling of fear was about me. These creatures gave off a dark vivid sense of power and death.

They had not seen me but now in the moonlight I caught a closer sight of one of them. The great beasts had huge tusks, curved around their massive mouths with a row of nasty sharp teeth. Their stout bodies were covered in great bristles and as they slavered, their red eyes flashed. Their feet ended in heavy sharp hooves.

I realised that they were wild boar. I had heard of these in stories told to Hamnet by his mother – these creatures that would attack a full grown man if provoked , beasts that grew to great size in the forest and ate smaller animals – animals like bear cubs!

Then one of them saw me! I carefully went to the far edge of the carrot pile, and grunted "Hello" in pig language, which greatly surprised the two boars.

"Do you mind if I eat?" I grunted.

The great boar stared at me with its narrow red eyes. "I suppose not, but keep to your end," it growled. I was happy to eat and say no more. There were enough carrots for all and soon we were all well fed.

The boars trotted off, making "We're going to sleep" noises. I followed them a little way behind. I watched them drink at a stream in the moonlight. I could tell the water was fresh and clean and I drank greatly of it until I could hardly waddle, so full was I of carrot and stream.

A little silver fish plopped up in the moonlight and then swam away again. I suddenly remembered how one day, when Master Shakespeare was writing, he looked up from his quill and paper and looked down at me. "Mummer," he said to me, musing,

" I write upon a dream …" Then he scratched my head and wrote, saying aloud, "Fear not, the boar will treat us kindly, you shall see."

After a while I saw the boars climb ungracefully through a hole into a huge hollow tree. As I crept nearer, a great smell of rotten apple came over me. I shivered – it was cold in the forest. I was a long way from my hearth. It would be warmer in that tree stump. I followed the boars inside and found them sleeping and snoring together. I curled up in the corner and soon was fast asleep myself.

I spent the next day in the forest, having awoken at dawn in the hollow tree to find myself alone, the huge boars gone. I was hungry and accustomed to being fed. For a while I was much distressed that I had no Hamnet to feed and hug me, but soon I smelt wild mushrooms and breakfasted upon them.

Then my nose led me to a sweet smelling tree where bees buzzed in and about. I remembered Master Shakespeare one day looking at me whilst I stood with my paws upon his silken clad knee as he wrote: "Where the bee sucks, there suck I." He paused, looked at me again and said, "In a cowslip's bell I lie …" By "where the bee sucks" I think he meant flowers, but the smell in that tree was too much for my nose. Overcome with senses and sweetness, nothing would suffice but that I must force my nose into the tree trunk, whereupon I sucked and licked the honey from the great bees' nest therein.

But my nose and tongue soon bore the pain of many stings as the bees stung me to protect their hoard. I brushed them aside with my paw before retreating toward the stream. My tongue was greatly swollen with the stings, but, soothed by the cool stream, my thoughts turned again to food. Then a strong smelling fish plopped out of the water and into my mouth. I was so astonished! My mouth still agape, I dropped the fish back into the stream and it swam away.

Then I heard some strange laughter. I stopped. There was a strange clanking noise – a man's noise, the noise of chains like those I had seen and heard upon the oxen in the farm. I smelt a strange yet sweet and friendly but frightening smell. Bear! The laughter was followed by a growl. "Oh, bless me, that's the first time I've laughed in a very long while," said a deep voice.

I looked around and there exhausted, his mighty head half covered with a leather and chainmail mask, lapping at the stream, lay a huge bear. Broken chains were still attached to its legs, and these had made the clinking noise I had heard.

"Help me, cub," he said, rattling his face mask. I chewed off the leather strap at the back of the mask. Then I followed the enormous ragged beast back down toward the stream. The great bear peered about for a moment in the darkening evening, then with his massive paws he smashed his legchain upon a rock by the stream. Now he was free. He caught some fish and shared them with me. As we ate, the huge bear told me his name was Stander,

"Thou art well struck in years," he said.

"What does that mean?" I asked

"Why, thou art a young cub and should see many summers," he proclaimed as he looked about the stream for more fishes.

I felt happy with him, even when, that night, the forest howled as a great tempest passed overhead and shook the ancient mighty trees. There were great whizzings and halations in the skies and the very earth trembled in a downpour of hard rain. Animals were scurrying and burrowing, and the birds had all taken flight in fear.

"Come, cub, the storm waits for no bear," growled Stander and led me upwards through the trees until great rocks appeared in front of us. I stumbled on behind Stander as he nimbly leapt upward until we were nearly atop the rocky hill that was hidden within the dark depths of the forest. There he ambled into a large cave and I followed him.

That night the rain lashed at the entrance of the cave, the mighty storm raged and trees crashed before the strong winds. Rain like icicle arrows spattered the edge of the cave and we moved deeper in. Stander lay down and dozed and I snuggled next to him for warmth, as he told me his terrible story.

25

Chapter Seven
Stander's Story

"I was brought up as a black bear cub in Russia. We were from a family of beautiful huge black bears who roamed wild in the woods. I learned much from my mother and played with my brother. They were happy times. My mother was strict and growled at us if we didn't stay close enough to her. She was worried about wolves. The Russian forests are full of packs of great grey wolves who prey hungrily on tasty bear cubs.

"One night we had been hearing wolves howl all day and we knew that a pack was closing in on us. We could smell them. My mother urged us to run faster with her and we did. But soon we became tired and, as we came to a clearing in the forest, there they were surrounding us. They were snarling, their red eyes glinting in the night, their fangs white, and their mouths dripping.

"My mother made us climb quickly up into a tree and then she stood in front of the tree, drawing herself up to her full height and shaking her head from side to side. Her back was to the tree and we watched down from the branches above. At first one wolf, bolder than the rest, came forward. The wolf growled, my mother growled, and then the wolf leapt. My mother dealt him a mighty blow with her great paw and knocked him across the clearing.

"For a while the wolves kept their distance, then again they came. This time two of them were snapping and snarling and leaping in and out, trying to bite mother. She grabbed them with her paws, bit them with her teeth, and flung them away. They fell, howling and crying. She swiped at the wolves with her mighty paws, tearing and clawing at them, and biting one after another. Yet still they came. More and more wolves closed in. Then some of the pack turned upon their own wounded wolves and started eating them even while they were still alive. Other wolves kept leaping and biting at my mother. Still more were circling around the tree, looking up at us and howling, their fangs bared.

"Below us Mother stood her ground and ripped and flung and fought and bit and tore at the wolves. Sometimes she killed one by grabbing it with both paws by the chest and tearing it apart. Immediately the other wolves stopped attacking Mother and fell upon the bloody corpse of their pack brother. My mother was blinded by blood; she had been hurt by the many bites of the wolves across her legs and belly. She fought all night, and as dawn came the wolves slunk away defeated and my mother – scratched, bitten, bloodied and exhausted – lay against the tree.

"We climbed down and gently began to lick her to help her feel better. Slowly, as light came, she dragged herself onward and her obedient cubs followed. When she was strong enough she led us away from that part of the forest and back up into the mountains. 'Never give in,' she said. 'Never give in, my cubs, remember you are the mightiest of creatures – a Bear!'

"It was a terrible journey as my mother bear was clearly tired and hurt from the fight. It rained and the wind howled and we climbed for hours. My mother went ahead of us and then rested by a huge rock. I turned back to search for my brother who could not keep up and to see if I could smell him as I could no longer see him. But looking for him I became separated from my mother.

"That's when it happened. A net fell over me and the more I struggled, the more the net tightened about me. I howled and cried. I had been caught by a woodsman. He took me in the net to a cart and from there we journeyed through the woods, with me struggling all the time in the net."

In the deep black night of the cave and the forest darkness, the big bear looked at me and sighed, as he said, "I never did see my beloved bear family again." He continued:

"Soon the trees thinned out and I could see that we were travelling through open countryside. We came to a great pair of gates with statues of winged eagles atop their posts. We went up a long drive through beautiful parkland and trees to a great house and into a cobbled yard where the horses' hooves spoke to the stones. Soon I was placed in a cage, still in my net. I struggled and fought and growled. I was fed some grey porridge and left to sleep. But I was still in my net and that night slept little. I prowled round the cage, reaching up, trying

27

the bars with my teeth, but it was no avail. I was hungry – the porridge had supplied little nourishment. I untangled myself from the net!

"In the morning the woodsman returned, this time with another man and two small children, a boy and a girl. The other man was short and plump, with twinkly eyes. He was wearing dazzlingly bright clothing. I could see he was friendly with the animals in their cages as he walked past them, stopping here and there with the children to give titbits to a zebra and pat its nose, or to slip something through the bars of the cage of a prowling angry ocelot from Arabia.

"The man talked the children and offered food to the animals, while behind them a servant carried a bucket of fruit. They arrived at my cage. 'Oh, he's only a baby!' cried the girl. 'Please, papa, can we keep him for a pet?'

"I wanted to put my head out of the cage and into the bucket that the servant held. I could smell a sweet fruit I had never known before. The girl, whose name I later learned was Annanelka, took a curved piece of fruit out of the basket and peeled off the leaves around it. She held it out near the cage. I went up to the narrow bars and very gently put my nose and tongue as far through them as I could. The little girl popped this sweet smelling fruit in my mouth. It was wonderful! Thus it was that I ate my first banana.

"And thus did I come to the Duke of Kamchatka's palace where I became a pet and plaything for the Duke's children. They had a zoo with many exotic animals. The duke's boy and girl loved me and petted me and fed me treats and sweetmeats. I played in the garden with them and I grew in the sunshine. I knew only kindness and gentleness from those children. I lived well and grew that year, my second year. But that summer the little girl died of a fever and all the house and zoo were closed. The duke went away to another of his palaces taking the little boy with him.

"I was a favourite among the keepers because I had been a cub with them but now with the duke gone and the house closed, came orders that the animals in the zoo were to be sold. For a long time the food was scarce and poor. Some of the zebras and camels were killed and fed to the lions. I ate some strange food then – I didn't always know what it was.

"Because I was a young bear and could do tricks with a ball, I was bought by traders from the Hanseatic league and sailed with them

28

across frightening choppy waters in their heavily laden boat. These men were traders between the German and Nordic lands and London. They spoke all the time of London, but that name meant nothing to me then. They had a dock of their own next to Savoy Court on the Thames. They kept me in a wooden cage with a feeding trap."

Stander paused to look at me and to see if I was still listening. But I was all agog to hear more, and he continued.

Chapter Eight
Stander in London

"London! The most dangerous place in the world for a bear, I had been well fed and well treated in the Duke's household and by then I was a very big, strong and happy bear. Humans had been good to me.

"But in London I was sold into the bear collection of Mr Philip Henslowe, the great bear-master!"

I asked Stander what a bear-master was. "Why, a showman," he replied. "A human who stages shows where bears fight. Now Mr Henslowe had the largest collection of bears in England – and the worst, most unhappy, group of bears they were. For Mr Henslowe owned the bear-pits, great open roofed houses with a huge space dug out and lined with wood.

"I soon learned that each night the bears were taken from their cages and put into the pits dug out of the ground – large deep pits, too high for even the tallest bear to climb out of. Around and above these, humans kept a screaming and drunken watch. And they would shout and cheer the dogs as they growled at the bears, wanting to attack them.

"I was taken out into the pit upon my second night there. I was chained to a post by a neckchain and iron collar and suddenly the trap of the pit on the side opened and a pack of screaming hungry dogs were let loose. They weren't chained and they came straight for me, leaping up to bite my face. I fended them off with my paws but still they came. I threw them across the pit but still they came snapping and howling and nipping and biting at me.

"I was frightened. Whichever way I turned and twisted, these vicious snarling slavering dogs were upon me, biting through my fur and into my flesh, snapping up at my legs and stomach, my arms and my nose! I became most angry and very quickly a power surged through me and nothing would do but I must attack them.

"I tore into those dogs, felling some with heavy blows of my paws and biting into some with my great teeth into their very necks. With my two paws I tore open the chests of others as blood spurted over us.

I bit through the necks of two more. This fight seemed to go on forever, but at last there was silence.

"There was nothing in the pit alive except me. In my angry mood I had killed them all.

"The crowd roared and Mr Henslowe and his handlers took me out of the pit with much laughing and 'Well done boy.' One of the handlers thrust a bucket of some strange sweet smelling brown liquid under my nose. I held it in my paws as I had been taught to do by the young Countess. And drained it dry.

"Mr Henslowe and his men cheered and filled me another bucket of beer which I also drank.

"Then they led me away from the pit to a small stream nearby. This I learned was a special place for washing wounded bears that had survived the pit.

"I heard one handler say, 'All seven dogs he killed. How he stood his ground! Aye he stands well.'

"And so my name became Stander. I was well looked after and well fed for about three weeks. I had not yet recovered of my wounds, but Henslowe's under bear-master, a man called Philpott, would put some stinging fluid upon my wounds that made me growl and lash out, but he had put me in a muzzle first."

I asked Stander what a muzzle was.

"Oh young cub, you should never know of one. It is a mask of leather and steel that humans put over your head, your bear's head, so that you may not bite. It is like the one you helped me out of, young cub."

We ventured out of the cave, as the rain had paused and we searched for food together.

The old bear looked at me kindly and continued.

"Bear men and bear handlers do it so as a bear may go out among the people and the people feel safe. Meantime, young bear, I would you climbed up into that tree." Stander gestured with his huge paw and arm at a mighty oak tree nearby. "You must climb the trunk first and then up unto those branches which are too light to bear my weight but will easily hold you firmly."

I did as the old bear bade me, climbing up happily into the mighty tree. Near the very top of the huge trunk the branches were smaller and I began to clamber about, clinging on to the branches and looking

31

for the giant green acorns there, for the winter was coming. I ate them with joy, while my clambering in the treetops dislodged many an acorn. Branchfuls fell loudly to the ground below, where Stander stood. He plucked a branch and began chewing the acorns, mouthing his thanks to me.

I clambered down to join him.

The sky was getting darker. "'Tis time we rested back in our cave," said Stander. "But let us eat these wild berries from this bush first. And methinks I hear bees buzzing nearby."

Above us the trees made a canopy under which we grazed. Soon we could hear the sounds of rain upon the leaves above us and distant thunder. We snuggled back up in the cave.

I thought of Stander's story. "I would have been so afraid," I said. Stander the great bear opened a weary eye, "I was," he said. "But many of the bear baiting fights are an illusion," said Stander.

"What is an illusion?" I asked.

He answered, "They are not true fights. They make a play thereof wherein they pretend that the bear has vanquished several great dogs, when in fact they be but mangy curs, the strong dogs withdrawn before they harm the bear. Thus the bear beats the dogs easily."

My eyes opened wide. "But then the humans do thus to save the bear," I said.

"Aye, 'tis true," replied the great Stander, "but it is for their own purposes, so that the bear may fight again and thus draw great crowds. Or pretend to fight again!"

I looked up at the older bear. Dawn was breaking outside the cave and light began to slip in to the darkness inside. "How can you tell whether they put you in a real fight?" I asked in my cublike way.

"If you are a famous bear, a bear of reckoning, a renowned bear of good repute, then needs must you becomes a most valuable prize, greater than perfumes of Araby, or fine cattle or even a small house. The value of a renowned bear becomes more than thrice three times his weight in jewels, gold and treasure, which the humans do prize, for it buys them their homes and food and horses and fine silk raiment. Thus they harm not the bear but make a stage for the fight, wherein the audience of cublings, grublings and groundlings think the bear fights but oft he does not so in truth. He acts as one upon a stage, for all the world's a stage and bears are merely players in it."

32

He continued, "Bears are stars in this Elizabethan age. Why even Good Queen Bess herself is much amused and enjoys greatly the baiting of a bear. Their names are as real in the mouths of the peoples and even of the Queen as are household words. Great renowned bears like *Blind Robin, George Stone, Bess of Bromley*, the mighty *Sackerson, Ned of Canterbury, Tom of Lincoln* or the great and giant bear *Harry Hunks,* are revered as famous fighters throughout the land. In London at the bear shows, people do come to see those bears and the bear men create fireworks which shoot whizzings and great halations in the sky. These cause many cries of 'Ooh' and 'Ah' among the populace. And the crowd roar and torches blaze and the trumpets blare and the bear is the gladiator and the great star who struts the stage of the pit to the roars and cheers of the crowd and the baying of the dogs. And the people drink beer and the bears are given beer."

Stander continued, "Why I myself had become one such bear, both for my size and my apparently fierce nature, though heaven knows violence is far from my mind. For I am a bear of peace. They fed me great numbers of eggs and ox hearts, milk and bread loaves, and sometimes a piece of sheep. To build up my strength I was rubbed down and washed by bearwardens; there are bear masters, bear keepers, bearlings and all sorts of other names among the humans for those who look after bears and do handle them. For bears are of great importance to England at this time. The men like Henslowe who stage the shows become rich, as do the men who own such bears as me. I was owned as part of Henslowe's grand and famous bear collection.

"But a bear can only be safe in his shows of strength for so long. Even if he is ageing it still seems that humans never do tire of the display and the violence and the snarling dogs and blood for themselves. However many bears die or are mauled, however many bears cunningly pulled from the fight, or the worst dogs pulled off them early to fill a wager – no sport is good enough, no fireworks bright enough, no blood from wounds that flow from the fur of a wounded bear crimson enough, but that a day will come for that bear to be beaten and killed by the dogs. Or the bears may be held cruelly in small cages among their own filth – unwashed, unlicked, unloved, like to a bear whelp abandoned by its mother.

"So I escaped," said Stander. "I bit through my leather strappings and bit the leg of my cruel handler who was transporting me away

33

from London to a show in Worcestershire, for I had dreamt that I should die in this show. Recalling this dream, I threw the cart over, broke out of my wooden cage, and ran into the woods. I ran for several days and became exhausted and poorly, as I would not hurt or hunt down a poor creature even such as a rabbit to feed myself.

"Now thou can come with me or return to thy loving family and enjoy their affection whilst thou art yet a cub. But if ever thou find that the children are gone from that house, that thou hast grown huge and waxed mighty and tall and very hungry, and the people no longer wish to feed thee every day at great expense, then beware! For they may sell or send thee to the bear-pits!

"And now I must move on deeper into the forest. Make thy choice, young cub, travel with me as a free bear or seek out thy ..." He interrupted himself, "Cublings, grublings and groundlings! I hear the voices of humans!"

Both of us listened carefully. The thin piping voice of a young boy called, "Mummer, Mummer, where art thou Mummer?"

"Why, it is my Hamnet!" I cried.

Chapter Nine
Reunited with Hamnet

So Stander watched as I rushed out of the cave, growling and squealing, and tumbled down the cliff. I could smell Hamnet and ran toward his voice. There in the clearing we were reunited and Hamnet cried, "Oh Mummer, thou art safe! I was afeard that thou wert dead!"

I could not even voice a growl but leapt up and hung tightly on to Hamnet, with tears in my eyes. Even Stander seemed to be moved, as I heard him say in bear language, "How much love do they both feel for each other!" And he turned away back into the forest. I mourned his going, but my heart was too warm for Hamnet for me to go with Stander.

"Come and let me see thee, young cub," cried Mistress Anne Shakespeare back at the cottage. And she poked and prodded me. "Poor bear, thou art covered in ticks and have already become thin. So fast hast thou lapped up much milk that I have sent for four buckets more! And look how I must mix up eggs and oats for thee, for thou wilt not touch the scraps of offal!"

Judith and Hamnet were so happy to see me again. They hugged me and played with me, and took me to the stream so they could wash me and pick thorns and insects from my fur.

"Aha," said Master Shakespeare. "The wanderer returns! The love of our hearth is better than the wild wood, methinks!" He leaned and tickled me and I licked his hand. Then I turned to nuzzle and lick Hamnet's face with great vigour.

"Such amity and such love hath thy savage beast, that were all the world honey and roses, he would forsake it for thee, Hamnet," quoth Master Shakespeare.

"We shall tame the savageness out of him, father," replied Hamnet.

"Somewhat we will," remarked Master Shakespeare, stroking his beard.

As Hamnet cuddled me and I nuzzled him, I sensed he was unhappy. I licked his face and this made him laugh out loud. "Oh Mummer, I am to go to Brasenose College in Oxford to be educated further and yet further, all too soon, when I am thirteen. Why I do not know! I can read, write, add and deduct. And know well my Psalms and, indeed, my father's writings." He snuggled me close and I licked his hand.

"Mistress Anne my mother and Master William my father think much about my future. But it all seems to be with wooden desks, tutors, and lessons under instruction, where I may not eat nor talk, and must sit or stand in dusty halls all the livelong day, whilst outside the sun shines brightly upon the paddocks and woods. And of course, dear Mummer," he looked at me, "They will not let me have a bear at Oxford. Though I were the Prince of England, they would not abide thee, my dear bear." He shook his head, and I shook mine as he had taught me.

He laughed and we wrestled upon the grass for a few sweet moments. "Would that Brasenose College were Bearsnose College for thee and me! Then therein I would roam in the woods and forests with thee and we should sup upon honey and pick wild berries and thou shouldst climb to the top of the tallest tree and throw down acorns as if I were your friend, the bear you were with in the forest – the old bear Stander whom I have heard that they still seek but cannot find. Yes, thou art educated already at Bearsnose college!"

We were interrupted from these musings by Mistress Anne calling Hamnet and Judith in for their supper. "And for goodness sake bring thee not that bear into the house but rest him outside in his place," she said sternly, showing her purpose by wagging her finger at me. "Methinks he may be still be covered in ticks and insects in spite of the wash you have given him. At after supper, thou shalt wash him yet more before he venture into the house!"

And sometime afterwards she brought me porridge in an iron bowl.

*** **

One day the Constable approached us and took us before the Town Clerk who issued a summons that Master William Shakespeare was to answer to the Aldermen as to why he endangered the populace by exhibiting a bear with no muzzle and no proper restraints. The Constable deemed that the very light chain which Hamnet had the blacksmith forge for me for three shillings (which his father paid), was "unsafe to hold a bear." So Master Shakespeare must before the

36

magistrates be brought upon charges that he as a showman did improperly exhibit a bear without the required lawful beast restraints.

Master Shakespeare put his hand upon Hamnet's head and said, "I stand here for this bear. I will say nothing more until before the Magistrate."

But Mistress Anne had much to say, sometimes crying out loud, sometimes muttering around the house. Many a "what a childish foolish boy Hamnet is to keep such a beast as a pet," did I hear her utter. "He will turn," she said, "That bear will be the ruin of us all, and we should rid ourselves of him."

"Oh no, Mother," protested Judith and Hamnet. "Dost thou not remember, Mama, how thou laughed one day when Father spake to thee when thou were complaining about the costs of feeding the bear?" said Judith. "Thou sayest, 'He will ruin us with his huge feeding! He is a huge feeder."

"Oh, a huge feeder," cried Master William, "why, thank you my sweet muse and morning star. I do much like that phrase." Mistress Anne blushed.

Master Will looked up from his manuscripts and made a note with his quill and laughed. As we all waited, he said to Hamnet, "The good Magistrate has recused himself as being such a friend and long time neighbour of the Shakespeare family. So we appear before the Clerk, my boy. Curiously, Master Fairdew is an even longer neighbour of the family and knew thy grandfather. He winked at Hamnet.

*** *

"Silence," was called, "The Clerk speaks."

The Clerk announced that he accepted the plea that the bear was a much loved pet bear, who had never hurt any person, and that Master Shakespeare was not exhibiting him, for which Master Shakespeare gave him thanks, while Hamnet hugged me quietly. Master Shakespeare agreed to pay a fine of five shillings and in future to keep me properly muzzled and chained should he bring me into Stratford-upon-Avon and the precincts thereof.

And in due course there came a time when I, a properly chained bear of the parish, came to market with young Master Hamnet. As soon as we entered the market place. a large dog lunged at me and I reared up, quite afraid. Hamnet dropped my heavy chain and happily, for my comfort, he had not fixed it too tight and it did slip off me, with my aid. Dogs were barking and people started screaming, so I blindly put my paw out and heard the tearing of cloth. It was a lady's dress. There were screams in the marketplace as I ran and knocked over the stalls in my panic.

But at last Hamnet recovered me, with the help of Will Greenaway, his neighbour's youngest lad. I was duly taken by the Constable before the Clerk again. Hamnet was presented with a two Pound fine! Or the bear to be destroyed! At this Hamnet did start to weep, and Mistress Anne was aghast. She said that this court fine and the matter of the bear (she would not say Mummer) was one for Master William. Hamnet knew not whether she was most upset about my fate or the two golden Pounds (a vast sum of money, a season's wages for a skilled workman). She laughed harshly and I suddenly understood the danger of my being sent before my time to heaven where bears must surely repose in great comfort and eat a lot.

Master William appealed the fine and argued that the bear had many times been into Stratford without incident, but the Clerk and the Aldermen were unmoved. "That creature groweth great in size and must therefore be judged to be a dangerous creature. If there is a third offence he is to be put down – destroyed."

Master Shakespeare paid the two Pounds as he could not abide the crying of Hamnet and Judith, but I think he also had a fondness for me. He loved me as I loved him. Thus I was not an early gift to the bears' heaven but happily came home with my family.

* * **

The spring was turning into summer. It was May 1595, the house was all abustle. A messenger had arrived at the gate, a strange man Hamnet and I had never seen before. We had been playing with Judith in the garden. He and his horse came in at the gatepost. He was behatted and wore a leather jerkin and did seem in great haste as he announced, "The theatres are to be opened again for the worst of plague hath abated."

Mistress Anne signed herself with the cross and muttered, "Thank the Lord. Suzanne, take the gentleman's horse. Come in sir, you must be tired and thirsty after your journey."

"Aye, and I bring letters from London for Master William Shakespeare."

As we were seated in the cottage I scratched lightly at the chain I must now perforce wear. "I have news," announced Mr Shakespeare, holding a parchment. "Mr Philip Henslowe has invited us to make with him presentations at the Rose Theatre in London. So we shall shortly travel there, Hamnet and I. We shall take some cloths and grain with us in carts to sell, so that we waste not a journey. We shall also send for Mr Greenaway and he shall provide a coach for us to ride in and some wagons to haul our packs thereof. I shall also take with me Ben Sharpe and two men from the village, most likely Mr. Greenaway's sons. They shall guard us therefore, since I shall also take with me to London much coin for the establishment of the theatre – its costumes, scenery, notices, lodging, fees, and messengers for the actors, guards and so forth. Much help has Mr Henslowe been to us concerning London, for as you know he has great shows and much spectacle there in the Paris Gardens. Thus 'tis settled."

"But what … what about Mummer?" asked Hamnet.

Mr. Shakespeare looked up at me.

"Methinks this sweet creature doth greatly grow and will be better accommodated in our great capital city. He shall ride with us."

Judith whispered to Hamnet, "Methinks Mummer hath grown exceeding large this last year."

"Why my son, he shall travel with us to London, it being deemed wise for him to leave Stratford in the light of his recent transgressions."

"You mean adventures, father," quoth Hamnet,

"Aye," said Judith, "for he is but a wild creature and cannot transgress."

"Yea, all he did was run amok in Stratford Market," said Mistress Anne, "and cause thy father to be fined two whole Pounds, and the bear sentenced or ordered 'to be disposed of'. Destroyed," quoth Mistress Anne.

"Yes, we all know," said Hamnet, covering my ears (but I heard through his covering hands).

"We are all agreed," said Master Shakespeare, "that it is best there be an escape made for this creature whilst he has life. But, children, the journey is not without hazard."

"There be rats!" cried Mistress Anne.

"Aye," said Master Shakespeare, "There be land rats …"

"And water rats!" chorused the children.

"There be water thieves and land thieves," cried Master Shakespeare and struck a dramatic pose in front of the bower.

Hamnet and Judith cried out together, "I mean pirates – pi-rats!"

And they all laughed. Hamnet was feeding me berries which I snuffled gently from his hand. The berries smelled sweet and enticing. How happy we were! I knew that this was my family. We frolicked in the garden of their home – my home.

"When do you go to London, father?" asked Judith.

"Why, upon St.Crispin's day," cried Hamnet.

"Or at least when we are all ready to travel," spoke Master Shakespeare.

"With such a great train!" added Mistress Anne sternly.

"Nay," said her husband, "It is with but a little train I travel, so that from the recent alarums there should no ill befall us upon the road. And Hamnet is to accompany me."

"And Mummer, too, please Father. You gave unto me your promise in this."

"Yes my dear Hamnet, and Mummer, thy companion of the growl. He shall rest upon my special wagon and you will ride with him. Long Harry will drive thee in the cart, I shall bring behind my horse and the wool wagons for which in London we shall see better coin than here where these woolly breeders, the sheep, are aplenty."

"What do they do with sheep in London, father?" asked Hamnet.

"They eat them, as do we! And we shear the wool from their backs here in Warwickshire, so that weavers of Axminster could make the cloth. Thy father's good friend hath collected the bales of wool and upon this venture all our ready use of treasure is risked. But we shall reach London sure and sell our wares. Your Mummer bear will earn his credit back by safeguarding our moveables. I have hired from Mr Greenaway horses and a carriage and two wagons for our journey, and four more horses and their feed. And the men who shall accompany us, good stout-hearted men known to me, Master Greenaway himself, and other trusted men who fought in the Flemish wars and know how to wield a sword, for they shall also work with me in London at our new playhouse, the Rose Theatre! A man must make a profit where he can."

"But father, you go not to London to sell wool."

There was a peal of laughter from Mistress Anne. "Thy father goes to London to enter into a great venture whereby we are to somewhat own our own theatre and thy father's plays will be shown there upon our own stage. A great company of men – actors, players that used to travel from village to village like unto a wandering troupe, now shall be settled in one place, in one auditorium where mirthful comic shows shall be the pleasure of the time. And, yea, the people shall come and pay their coin aplenty to see and hear our merry tricks. For Mr Philip Henslowe has newly built a great theatre called the Rose and we are to be merchant adventurers with him."

That name again! I remembered it from Stander's tales about the bear-pits and Mr Henslowe the Master of The Queen's Bears, a cruel bearmaster who set packs of hungry dogs upon bears to fight them. All this so the people should arouse their worst passions and drink and gamble and scream to see such beautiful creatures cruelly ruined. Bears were blinded, and then whipped, all for this terrible savage humour of crowds, Stander had told me. And I was sore afraid. I trembled.

Hamnet sensed my terror. He hugged me and said "but thou Mummer art destined for the theatre! The Rose of London!"

Mr. Shakespeare said, "We shall make our fortunes from this wooden O!"

Mistress Anne was excited. "The public will shower thy father with gold and silver yet – and even the copper coins from the groundlings who pay but a penny will all help our fortune. The new playhouses of London, England's great capital, will make thy father, Master William Shakespeare, one of England's richest citizens!"

"Her Majesty's players shall play his plays, and the great Queen Elizabeth shall rejoice to see the histories of her forbears!" said Susanna.

"Yes," said Mistress Anne, "And both Her Majesty the Queen, with her nobility and courtiers, and the common people who pay in copper and silver coin will be thus entertained. Why a farmer with thrice three dozen acres could not see so much coin, nor a noble Duke prise from his poor tenants in a year as much, as the theatre will bring to thy father!"

"I pray that it shall be so," said Susanna.

41

"He will also buy cloths, sheep, grain and even dwelling houses – and thus shall we thrive!"

"Aye and so shall our partner, Master Philip Henslowe," added Master Shakespeare.

Mistress Anne was concerned, "What Henslowe, the bear-pit man? He makes creatures fight for sport."

"Yes and the public does adore the show. If our plays took only half and even half again, of what Mr Henslowe takes, we would do well, for he is a shrewd business man, albeit slow to pay his debts!"

"To set savage packs of dogs to bait a poor creature like a bear," said Hamnet, holding me tight, "'Tis cruel. It makes us no better than savage beasts – nay worse, for men do this for sport while beasts only kill for food."

Mistress Anne was disgusted. "It is cruel! Therefore let the public flock to thy father's battles and wars and tempests, murder and treachery, where all the players come home safe at the end of the play, then do make most merry in the taverns – even if they have acted death upon a stage."

"Shall Mummer do his tricks, father?" asked Hamnet, and his father said aye.

"But what if Mr. Henslowe takes a fancy to him when I am back at school in Stratford? Wilt thou promise me …"

His father interrupted, "I know how much love for that creature is in your heart. Fear not, sweet my son. That bear is yours and you have taught him well to play. What you learned from Mr. Banks and Morocco will stand thee and him in good stead. I promise thee that Mummer shall not be baited – he is too young a cub …"

"And when he is older?" asked Hamnet, still worried.

"Not even then," said Master Shakespeare, "for then he shall strut the stage and play Caesar."

They all laughed and Hamnet bade me "Up." I stood upon my hind legs with my paws out and Hamnet put a cloth of fine silk about my shoulder and bade me walk, the which I did upright, holding out one paw with the cloth.

"He is a fine actor," said Mistress Shakespeare.

"He is a Mummer, for he doth not speak," said Judith.

"Aye, but he can growl and grunt and click his tongue and sometimes roar," said Master Shakespeare.

"He cannot roar yet – he is but a cub. Albeit he is becoming a larger one," said Judith.

But Hamnet gave me a secret signal and I roared! All drew away in fright, but Hamnet burst out laughing.

Master Shakespeare said to his wife, "We must to London, while thou wilt hold our hearth and home for us here in Stratford. As I have told thee:

There is a tide in the affairs of men.
Which, taken at the flood, leads on to fortune;
Omitted, all the voyage of their life
Is bound in shallows and in miseries.
On such a full sea are we now afloat,
And we must take the current when it serves,
Or lose our ventures."

Thus it was that we set out one fine spring day from Stratford to London, the greatest city of the realm, wherein Master Shakespeare was to present his plays.

43

Chapter 10
Travel to London

Everyone was greatly excited when the packhorses and wagons were prepared that would transport Master Shakespeare and his party – which included Hamnet – to London. There was much discussion about Hamnet's schooling whilst he was to be away – he must not be allowed to fall behind his classmates, but London would be a great education for him, as his father told him.

That spring Hamnet and I wrestled and played, Judith fed me sweets and all I knew was much kindness and love from these children. They had not a dark thought within their hearts and they loved me as deeply as I loved them in return. We three cuddled and hugged and nipped and played like unto three bear cubs. And Master Will, with his arm around Mistress Anne, would stand there laughing, a happy sound to my bear's ears.

But I could not help but recall Stander's words to me: "London is the worst place in England in this worst of times for bears, for they are put to fight packs of dogs. The dogs leap loose whilst the bear is tied chained to a stake." And Mistress Anne her very self had said of their Good Queen Bess, that " she enjoyed to bait bears to the death. So I could not but fear the great hordes of the raucous populace – vagabonds and drunkards, with their vermin!"

"Yet London is a fine and a fit place for actors," said Master Shakespeare.

"And bears?" asked Hamnet.

"Aye, and for bears too!"

"But we shall not bait Mummer, father! Thou hast sworn …"

"Nay, for he has had his savageness loved out of him," his father reassured him – and me!

"And he has been fed," said Mistress Anne, "and fed again! He shall serve thee well, this bear!"

"And so shall I," said Hamnet.

"And so ye shall," Master Shakespeare insisted, "for you have trained him. For not only shall this bear assist in the theatre where a

44

wild bear would not be safe. But he shall also honestly and faithfully guard our rich moveables, as he hath no desire for gold and silver. He loves much food and sweet berries and to have his titbits from thee when thou dost thy tricks with him."

"Aye, he will guard our gold coin too," said Hamnet, puffing out his chest to make himself look bigger than he was.

"But what if robbers – land rats! – should assail thee upon the road, father?" asked Judith with a worried look.

"Soon I will show you what we shall do," said her father.

Some days passed during which there was a great hammering as a cage with iron bars and a great wooden base and roof was made for me to travel in. We all trooped to the wagon whereon was this stout iron cage, and Master Shakespeare slid back a wooden plank in the floor of my new den. "There is a space here below," he showed them.

"Under Mummer!" cried Hamnet.

"Yes, who shall risk to disturb a bear? You well know how Mummer growls and flails if you trouble him when he sleeps or eats. So he shall play Caesar and he shall guard our fortunes also."

Though it looked fearsome, the cage was spacious, and it had a boxed den for me to snuggle up in and go to sleep.

"But Mummer needs not those iron bars, father, for he is a sweet natured bear," said Hamnet.

"Mummer may not need bars of steel, but I do! Forsooth behold what the Jewish clockmaker Levi hath made – this casket of lead to lie in a secret compartment under Mummer's cage." He slid back the floor and showed them the casket, wherein were golden ducats and notes to Italian bankers in the city as well as much silver coin. "Make Mummer familiar with his carriage and thus shall he sleep upon our fortunes, our movables, and guard them well, as if they were his own. Aye, if he is comfortable within his cage, he will not let strangers too close – or he will growl, as Hamnet has taught him."

"Yes, Mummer shall growl upon his cue," said Hamnet. "He stands and roars upon his cue."

"And nibbles raspberries gracefully from my hand, father," said Judith.

The whole family laughed, as Hamnet talked to me as he would talk to his sister. "Mummer," he said, "these are most wonderful times."

"Yes," said his father, "there are great advances in science and art, there are ships being built and traded and new worlds to be discovered."

** ***

The land was busy as we travelled the road to London. Many people turned and looked at us, for we were indeed a show. Arthur and Hal, Master Shakespeare's two horseriders, went ahead of us, with swords and daggers at their waists. Their horses were fine strong beasts as I knew well, for one kicked me when all I did was try to befriend it. I stayed clear of these creatures as I could not understand them.They were not kind and companionable like Morocco!

Thus we prepared to embark upon our great and long anticipated journey to London, taking goods to trade, and, even more important, plays to act in the theatre that awaited us. We were bringing costumes and wagons to the Rose Theatre that had been promised to Mr Shakespeare, in partnership with Master Philip Henslowe, the great impressario who organised spectacles with fireworks, musicians, actors and those who performed mock jousts.

I was travelling in my great cage, though for a while I could ride with Hamnet up in the carriage behind the two drivers. Upon our wagon and the one behind were heaped many sheep's fleeces to sell in London. Some passers-by stood in shock when they saw me, so after some oncoming horses had reared up, Master Shakespeare ordered Hamnet to set me back in my cage.

The procession was headed by Tham and Jack, Mr Greenaway's two tall sons, each astride a stallion. These horses were spare haulers for the carriage and likely would be sold in London.

The people stared, seeing first the men on horseback, then the great wagon of cloths and goods pulled by four horses, and then our great wagon of props and clothes, and Master Shakespeare's great closed carriage, drawn by two black horses. "It is a carriage good enough for the Queen herself," said Master Greenaway. He and Master Shakespeare together had had some part in the making thereof – this fine burnished wooden carriage, dark and smart with windows and a door at either side. It was in there they travelled, like princes or great ambassadors. Then behind the carriage was our wagon, with myself in my fine cage, pulled by a further four horses. I sat in my cage of iron freshly made by the blacksmith in Stratford. I had straw in a corner

46

wherein I lay sheltered from view. Hamnet chose often to sit with the two men who drove our wagon, the heaviest of the cavalcade.

Sometimes, when we halted away from the villages, Hamnet took me out of the cage, still upon a light chain and leather collar, and walked a while with me, feeding me titbits whilst I sniffed and smelt the wonderful air, the scents of the flowers, and the strange animal smells.

This then was our first day. Then the sky grew darker and there were slight spots of rain and Master Greenaway did propose that the Shakespeare party should take lodgings and rest. So Hamnet told me that we were soon going to stop for the night. That night we lodged at the White Hart Inn near to Henley-in-Arden, only some twelve miles from our starting point, a place Mr Greenaway knew well. Again all was action as our men saw the horses down for the night and drew the wagons tightly together in the yard of the coaching inn.

The landlord and maids jollied about welcoming the party, showing the men to the roustabout quarters. Then the landlord spoke quietly to Master Greenaway, and he approached Master Shakespeare. "'Tis two shillings for the bear, Master Will!"

"Two shillings for the bear! I could bed down myself for that!" fumed Master Shakespeare. "'Tis four days wage for a skilled man!"

Master Greenaway continued. "Aye, that is not to bed him. We must pay to have him for the night about the Inn, and he must not be taken from his cage other than to clean it."

Master Shakespeare spoke quietly to his son. "So Hamnet, one of the men will help you clean the bear's cage and lay for him fresh straw. Remember that at all times thou art to stay close by the cage with the bear, that our golden purse shall be safe beneath the floorboards of the creature's carriage."

"Call him Mummer, father, not a creature! His name is Mummer!"

"Aye," said Master Will, " and right well named he is, for he struts and walks and prowls and growls like an actor – a mute actor like unto the mummers we saw alongside the jesters and jugglers when that party came to Stratford-upon-Avon last Easter with their mirthful comic shows."

And so Hamnet and the ostler's man carefully swept out and washed my cage, laid fresh straw and then locked the cage up. I was a happy bear, a bear of great content in that I had the love of my master

Hamnet Shakespeare, and the love also of his renowned family, even if the matriarch good Mistress Anne scolded me when I came into the house from the garden.

****

I slept. I dreamt. Suddenly I awoke and heard the sounds of the forest beyond the yard of the Inn wherein Hamnet slept. I was aware of the sweet smells of the forest, the scent of the night flowers, the odour of the horses ... My eyes snapped open. The pungent smell of bear. Bear! Yes I was awake and could smell the stink of bear. Stander! And there he was at the edge of my cage, gasping, heaving. I happily passed him fruit pieces and my wooden bowl of water, resting them upon a ledge at the edge of the cage where was my feeding space in the bars. The cage was made of iron bars welded across each other to make small square windows. At the corner of each iron square was a crossed spike, reaching almost to the centre of the squares. The cage was a very strong and heavy and was impossible to get into or out of, without the key! But Hamnet and I had a secret.

Stander stuffed the fruit into his mouth most readily and greedily, slurping and sucking at the water.

"Young cub," said Stander, "young Mummer, whither goest thou?"

"To London, my old friend" I replied. "There to join my masters in the making of shows, with Master Shakespeare and Master Philip Henslowe."

Stander rattled my cage angrily. "Nay, thou must not go! They will bait thee and blind thee and whip thee in what they ill do call sport. Henslowe! He is the worst man in England and rules the hell of bears that is London. Thou must fly hence now with me into the forest. I have known by smell for a while that thou were here and thus have come toward thee."

"But I cannot leave!" I protested.

"I will soon have this cage open," growled Stander.

"I am not to be baited. Hamnet hath promised me!"

"He loveth thee 'tis true, but he is but a child. Neither you nor he know of the dreadful fate that awaits thee in the bear-pits of London. Vicious dogs, men who whip thee for sport and packs of hounds who fight and bite at thee whilst thou art chained to a stake. The men who will bet upon thee to thy death. I would kill Henslowe were I to get my claws on him." The huge bear shuffled to his feet. Stander looked upon the windows of the Inn and I believed that he meant to enter therein. "Is he here? Sleeps he here among the company tonight? Which is his horse?"

"Nay he rides not with us," I said. "And those therein would be terrified of thee and like to use pistols," I murmured strongly.

"But thou thyself must leave now and be safe," Stander answered. "There is no promise a human can make to a bear except suffering and death – aye and that right slowly." The old bear snarled.

Just then Hamnet appeared and Stander reared up his head, shaking from side to side. Hamnet reached below the cage, opened the shelf therein and brought out a bowl of porridge mixed with milk for my breakfast.

"No one will harm thee, great bear," said Hamnet.

I smelt the food, and then Hamnet gave it to Stander! I was both angry and pleased. Then Stander sank down and as Hamnet backed away from the bowl did the great bear stoop and eat of the porridge. Hamnet reached up to the cage and tapped it in our special signal. I crossed the cage and, reaching down, moved the hidden secret lever set in the wood. "This is my escape should there ever be need," I told Stander. I moved the iron and with a click opened a small door on the other side. I scrambled over, slid back the iron cage door, and moved through the gap to join Hamnet. He was passing out whole fruits to Stander, who conveyed to me an apple, which I munched. Hamnet watched us, not understanding whereof we spoke as bears.

"So," said Stander when he had finished eating, and as Hamnet poured him more water, "You could have got out of the cage and come with me into the forest by yourself, yet you stay."

Hamnet looked on as we bears grunted and growled in our conversation. He moved softly about the perimeter of the cage, looking around, but all was quiet. Soon Stander and I made our farewells and I scampered back into the cage and Hamnet pressed the secret lever down and locked it. Thus was my night at the White Hart Inn. Soon I could no longer smell Stander.

** * *

In the morning there was much bustle as the ostlers moved through the yard, rousing and feeding the horses. Hamnet came late to feed me and open out my cage so I might stretch my legs and the waste be thrown away, and fresh straw put there by the lads for the journey.

49

After I had eaten and been watered, we wandered into the woods, with me upon my light chain. I sniffed around. There were butterflies, flowers, trees, leaves, shrubs, rabbits … But no Stander.

On that next day of our travel the clouds that had lour'd about us now burst forth, showering us with rain. Some four miles since we had left the White Hart at dawn we had made little progress. That night we were to stay as guests of my Lord Makepeace, but we wondered if we would ever get there, so hard did the rains pour down and in such force that the heavens opened and there was like unto a flood. Sheets of rain drenched us all and Hamnet was shivering and soaking wet. I could not move to shake my fur free of the water which had blasted in and poured through my little home. As we moved slowly on, a rider upon a black horse joined us and proceeded to ride some time with us as we rolled along the rainracked drenched stormy lanes. He then tied his horse to the back and rode in Master Shakespeare's closed carriage, whilst I was pleased that Hamnet sat with me, though even under his sheepskins he was very wet and cold.

On that second day we were struck again and dashed again by storms, and that so fiercely that the horses were affrighted and the great wagon of wool skidded into the ditch. "We are not Noah in his Ark," cried Master Shakespeare, drenched once he was out of the carriage and directing the men to lift the stuck wagon. Then the wagon I was in fell suddenly, its front sinking down into a ditch. I was now perilously housed, as my cage had tilted on to its end as the wagon slid into the great ditch. From thence in the rain Master Greenaway and his lads tried mightily to pull the cart out, but eventually it had to be unloaded. Gently Hamnet unlocked my cage from the sinking wagon, and, putting my light chain upon me, brought me out to stretch and breathe. I was as wet and soaking a furred beast as any you have ever seen!

We took shelter in the part of the forest among the nearby trees. There was an old charcoal burners' hut, and there around a fire the men rested, wrapped up in leathers. Hamnet fed me some cold potage he had in a leather bucket, and Master Will talked with the men and then spoke to Hamnet: "Master Greenaway and I are moving on with our carriage and one wagon. We will ride ahead to the house of Lord Makepeace. Master Greenaway's lads will stay here with you, Hamnet, whilst this wagon is being repaired and the cage reloaded.

Then you will join us. Take care of the wagon and its goods, stray not too far from that sunken cage."

Master Shakespeare gestured at the ditch and continued. "Another lad, Shep, will be here to look for you, from Master Greenaway. It is the lad who rode behind us with a small cart – he will be here upon the road soon. Master Greenaway's sons will try to repair the big wagon and get you all back upon the road. And Hamnet, look specially to that bear's cage, my leaden casket, and the moveables therein. Stray not from them, my son, and also keep your bear close to the cage until it is repaired and fixed back again atop the wagon. This box shall I take with me." So saying did Master Shakespeare pick up a wooden box which seemed heavy. Then he left in the great closed carriage, We watched the lantern upon the carriage until it was out of sight.

Hamnet walked me out on a light chain just a few yards, to the very edge of the forest. Suddenly I was beset with a smell. Growling I pulled back toward the cage. "Ah yes, Hamnet," came the voice of Master Will, who was standing under a tree. "Whence dost thou take Mummer after I had asked thee to stay near the cage?"

Hamnet answered, "This far and no further – we are but a few steps from the cage, yet Mummer may feel more free."

"Dost thou care less for my treasures,son than for thy bear's feelings?"

Hamnet did not answer but we walked back to the cage.

"Mummer seems anxious," said Long Harry, the wagon driver. "His great nose is sniffing the night air."

Bear, I could smell bear – and not just any bear! I could still smell Stander! Stander was nearby!

Chapter 11
Robert Cecil Visits Lord Makepeace's House

At last the rain abated and the carts were mended, so we continued that afternoon upon our journey to the magnificent country home of Lord Makepeace. My cage was placed in the courtyard and I was loosed to be fed and watered, as were the horses. In the yard I had been startled by a group of men who suddenly appeared. One was riding and the rest walked their horses into the courtyard, hooves clattering upon the cobblestones. The rider at their head was a small hunchbacked man. He bent over as a groom aided him to dismount from his steed, and there he stood. The visitors were all hailed and well met by servants, and their horses were led away. They stretched themselves as they were shown into the house.

Hamnet rushed, with me scampering at his heels, to tell his father, "I saw a strange small bent over man arrive on horseback, accompanied by a platoon of soldiers armed with muskets."

"Ah," said his father, "This is the one whom we were expecting."

"Look after the soldiers in the servants' quarters," said Lord Makepeace. "My household has prepared the main guest room for our distinguished guest."

That evening Hamnet and I performed some tricks to entertain the noble company whilst they dined. There was much applause and many compliments to Hamnet for the comic and mirthful show. After supper we all sat in the Great Hall of Lord Makepeace's mansion. The ladies bade us goodnight, and Hamnet and I lay quiet whilst the men lit their pipes. Then the door opened and the man I had seen, of small stature but richly dressed, entered the room. He was introduced to the small assembled company of nobles by Master Shakespeare: " Gentlemen, this is Robert Cecil, the younger son of William Cecil, first Baron Burghley. And the philosopher Francis Bacon is his close cousin."

The people greeted him and made space for him. He was small and bent, but to my bear's mind he seemed to have power. Shakespeare whispered, "Our age loves beauty in men and women, so that Robert Cecil, for all that he is a brilliant governor, endures much spite for the way he appears."

Lord Makepeace whispered back, " He suffers much ridicule accordingly – our revered Queen Elizabeth calls him 'my pygmy'! His father, Lord Burghley, fond of both his sons, once said that his son Robert could rule England, but his son Thomas could hardly rule a tennis court."

They both laughed, and Lord Makepeace continued, "But this Cecil is not thought upon lightly by the Queen, nor by none in this house and realm. He is of great import, clever, and is spoken of as the most powerful man in England. Since the death of Francis Walsingham he is, as you know, William, charged with being the queen's chief intelligencer-spymaster." He put down his napkin and rose from his chair, and at this sign the company rose. Lord Makepeace and the diners made their farewells and left the room.

Master Cecil seated himself with Master Shakespeare and wine was brought to them. Hamnet and I sat quietly in the shadows as the firelight flickered. "So, Master William," said Robert Cecil, "thou art in favour with the Queen, and thou art welcomed in all households, whether the masters be friendly to the Queen or not?"

William looked uneasy.

"Soft, Will, I have little of my father's bigotry or religious zeal. My zeal is for the Queen and her wellbeing." Cecil paused.

"As in truth is mine own," said William.

Cecil resumed. "Indeed and so it is. In these dangerous times, we lean toward a tottering state. There are a great many foreign plots and conspiracies that purpose the death of our sovereign, Good Queen Bess. In this uncertain world, thou canst, I hope, be of service to her Majesty."

"Speak and I shall obey," said William.

"Thou hast a great talent, a gift for the telling of tales, and do hold great mastery of the Queen's English, and the performing of plays of history with its great battles and persons replicated upon thy stage, to the delight of the populace. Thus far, as a playwright and an actor, but also as a citizen of the realm and a subject of her Majesty, thou stands well with aristocrats, with men of the city, with the nobility and the men of influence. Thou art blessed with great and wondrous abilities to make shows and tell the tale.

"As I told thee when we last met, I want thee to enhance and give advantages to the true story of Richard, the Third of that name, and to dwell upon his villainy to his own brothers, his murder of the princes in the tower, his unworthiness to be king, the ploys and complots he used to get there, the faults of his lineage ..."

Master William interrupted Cecil, "I have here my manuscript, reformed a second time," he said and passed it to Cecil, who read for while and we were all silent.

"Aha, that's the stuff," said Cecil. "You have Richard saying 'If I cannot prove the lover I shall play the villain!'" And he slapped his thigh, folded the document and put it into his large velvet pouch. "I shall read it in my chamber tonight with pleasure!"

"You commanded me to write that earlier play, The History of King John which I did, but for reasons known to you it has not been staged."

Cecil interrupted, "Nor maybe never will yet, but let it rest for now. May hap it shall have its moment in the sun, but meantime we need to show that the last Plantagenet King, Richard the Third, usurped the throne, murdered his nephews and turned England into a slaughterhouse for all who opposed him. We need to show that the Queen's grandfather, Henry the seventh of that name, held the throne by right, through his mother Mistress Beaufort, and that the Tudor line doth righteously rule England."

I yawned, not understanding whereof they spoke, but Hamnet listened attentively in the shadow, and slipped me a sweetmeat. Cecil glanced over to us.

"That is thy son Hamnet, is it not?"

"Yes, my Lord."

"And a good time of evening unto you, Hamnet. After supper is my favourite time. But what's this? You have a bear?" "Yes, Sir Robert," said Hamnet, "and a friendly, tamed and kind-natured bear is he."

"Yes, when you made the show earlier for the company, I was observing quietly from the gallery, I saw how faithfully he obeys you, and how fiercely his gaze is upon thee! You entertained the company most excellently, sirrah," said Cecil.

"Thank you, Sir Robert."

"Would he take a piece of fruit from my hand?"

"Why certainly, Sir Robert, said Hamnet. "His name is Mummer." He bade me gently forward to where our visitor held out a piece of apple.

"Place it in the flat of your hand, Good Sir" requested Hamnet of Cecil.

Cecil put his hand out flat with the apple in the middle. "Here, Mummer," he said. Gently I lowered my head and scooped the morsel up with my tongue.

"How gentle he is! Indeed, Hamnet, thou hath schooled him well."

"You are most gracious, Sir Robert." replied Hamnet.

Cecil returned to his politics. "We need much to fortify the true and legitimate Queen and the House of Tudor and their true rights to the throne – her true and honest lineage, her favour by the Almighty, and Richard the third, his strange birth ,so on and so forth. To do this we must also show the illegitimate and wicked reign that preceded the accession of the House of Tudor. Thou tells a tale that we will weave into History"

"Somewhat we will" Cecil continued

As well as thy writing and listening talents, we have need for thy honesty. There is a small fortune in movables to be transported to our treasury man in London. In the morning my men shall give these to you in chest and pouch. At my command did one Philip Henslowe approach thee and at my command doth seek thee out as a partner and shall assist thee."

"I am grateful and honoured."

"Henslowe, with whom you are now acquainted and familiar, hath built anew, with the secret purse, a theatre, the Rose, and you will perform there. But thou knowest all this already."

"I knew not that Henslowe was in thy service."

"He is a rude crass shrewd villain, yet he is our shrewd villain, and he performs for us many secret and important deeds south of the Thames river. Now will he further support thee, with thy company of players. All this so far is from the Queen, who wishes you well. Now this is from myself – take care, for there are Spanish plots afoot to kill the queen. Whilst they are many, only one needs to succeed to cause her death, so we need to foil them all. There is unrest and hidden conflict. I visit to enlist you – to discover whether you will or no to be in the service of the Crown, and to inform and advise me of any plots against her majesty,

since you may more easily than I enter into the presence of those who plot. The Queen recognizes and cherishes your great worth and loyalty along with the measure of your mirthful comic shows and great tragedies. Your fine plays are accepted and your talent – she enjoys your work, which hath flourished the more."

"I enter her service with true heart. So thrive I," said Master Shakespeare.

* * * *

I could smell London a long way before we came near to the Thames at Richmond, upon the north bank. Hamnet talked excitedly with Tam the cart driver and his companion Giles Greenaway, Tam's cousin, who had joined them at Oxford. He was a large quiet man of whom I was somewhat nervous. Now the fields gave way to cottages lining the road, and a huge movement of travelers surrounded us , inching their way through mud and cart-jam to the city. Master Shakespeare rode ahead in his carriage and sometimes Hamnet would join him there for a while. Hamnet told me His father was muttering aloud his newly written words as the wagon wheels of the carriage bumped jerkily over the stony road.

For a long while I slept. I was dreaming about being held and cuddled by Hamnet, and of the hogs in the forest – but also of Judith's peals of laughter when I ran away because I had been frightened by her puppy. Then I remembered the words – "To sleep, perchance to dream ..." – that Master William had uttered once when he was feeding me titbits of fruit and I had dozed off. He often uttered odd sayings like this, and then would write them down in his great book. When Hamnet asked him, his father said they might come in useful sometime! I had had lovely dreams while we were on the way to London, of smelling the boars and the food scraps among the hollow trees in the forest, and Hamnet calling me, as he and Judith playfully ran across the meadow chasing me in the bright sunlight.

Chapter 12
Paris Gardens!

Then came a great noise and I awoke. We were in London – and we were near to Henslowe, that man Stander had told me about, who ran the bear-pits! To my dismay, I learned from listening to Hamnet and his father that I must lodge with the fighting and baited bears at the Paris Gardens bear-pit, until the house where the Shakespeares were to stay, the Old Moor's house by the river, was ready to accommodate us. The Shakespeares and their entourage were to stay at an Inn nearby. So there was the news I dreaded: I was to join the bears at the bear-pits – my greatest fear!

When they took me to the bear-pit, Hamnet told his father that I would be afraid, but Master Shakespeare tried to comfort him. "Nothing shall happen to Mummer. Until the Old Moor's house is ready, so we must stay at the Bankside Inn, and some of our party will be at the Old John public house. But it will only be for a few days. Mummer must perforce lodge at the Mr. Henslowe's bear garden, as Henslowe has agreed to take him, and Henslowe's men will care for Mummer's needs. There is no room for him at the Inn, nor is it permitted to house a wild bear here in the midst of Southwark."

"But he is not wild, father!" Hamnet cried.

I myself was much afraid, as I sensed Hamnet's fears. As we drew close to the Paris Gardens I could hear the pain filled howls and distressed growls of bears. I recognised their great sadness in their misfortune, and I could smell their fear. We walked down a tunnel of stone behind two of Mr. Henslowe's bear attendants, while our shadows flickered upon the walls from the flaming torches the men bore. I felt icy cold. And as the great iron studded wooden door opened I was overwhelmed by the smells, the unhappy stench of blood, pain and death.

"You have overruled my wishes but not my mind, father," said Hamnet. His father only said, "Never fear, thy beloved bear will be safe and well kept for these days. I would not make thee unhappy, my son."

"But Mummer is so frightened, father! See how he shivers in fear and his eyes stare!"

"Methinks the cries of the other bears do trouble him, but all will be well with him, my son"

"Here sir," said one of the bear-men, guiding us in. With a heavy chain part muzzle and my eyes half-blinded by cloth, I was dragged against my will down a tunnel covered with brick, stained dark up to half its height, and scarce enough wide for two parties to pass each other. The man leading us said, "This was an old cave in the chalk rock of Southwark and Mr. Henslowe has made the tunnel down toward this bear-holding chamber."

Then we came out into a larger area with a wooden roof high above us. We entered a many-arched and bricked chamber underground wherein were many cages dark against the walls in the flickering torchlight. Even in the poor light, I could make out how inside the cages bears were pacing restlessly, their heads shaking from side to side. I could hear their moans and smell their fear. I had never seen such desperate, unhappy and unquiet tortured creatures. These were my fellow bears and I was sore afraid. It became strangely silent yet as we passed into the chamber and the bears followed our progress , Then the unhappy moans did start again. I saw now and heard many bears who, as bears will, started growling and whining to each other. In truth I perceived that their growls meant sadness, fright and pain, and foretold death.

Then I was led toward a small solitary cage near a ramp which seemed to lead back upward to the hall above us. I was still muzzled, and perceived that many bears were muzzled like me. This discomfort of a leather and iron framework about my mouth and head was a double prison, right close upon my nose and face. All the time I was in pain and unhappiness and scarce could breathe. Some bears shared cages and a few others were chained to the very walls of their solitary prison cages of iron bars hard against the walls, so that they could scarcely either lie or sit. Then I perceived that there were dogs in a great tunnel adjoining us, much better lit and with more men present. I smelt them and heard barking as the yowling dogs were separated from us by but a wooden gate.

Around midday the men began to feed some of the bears, and to put fresh straw down. Then the dogs too began to awake and to snarl and bark fiercely. The bears nearby shrank back from them. I could only but partly see because of my head being rudely wrapped with that stinking and drenched cloth. But from the corner as I tilted my head back a ragged gap afforded me a view of the place I had hoped never to see or be imprisoned in.

We were in the stone dungeons of Paris Gardens, London, the world's busiest and most dangerous bear-baiting arena. Above us were wooden areas that housed the pits wherein bears were chained to the stake. Near me I saw a huge dark bear, bigger yet than Stander. He moved about in his cage, not chained to the wall and without a muzzle. Food and water he had in his cage and he eyed me warily. He was truly a huge bear, like a throwback to an ancient era, he was truly a giant .

The day passed slowly. I was in a cage by myself among other cages and quite near the baiting pit. It became quiet and most bears seemed to be asleep so I dozed off. Then two men came toward me and I perceived that one was Hamnet! My heart leapt.

"He needs no muzzle in here," said Hamnet, slipping the man a coin. I caught a glint thereof in the firelight as the man took it in his hand and unlocked my cage.

Hamnet was with me now and I hugged and embraced him, as if never would I let him go. His sweet smell filled my nostrils, and tears flooded my eyes. "Oh thou poor babe!" groaned Hamnet as he uttered soothing words to me. "Thou poor, poor bear, what have they done to thee?" Gently he unstrapped the muzzle and passed it out to the attendant who had now been joined by others. They watched as Hamnet and I embraced.

Hamnet snapped his fingers and one man passed him up a bowl of water which he placed gently before me. I lapped it greedily, hardly daring to leave his embrace. "There there, dear bear, fear not," he said to me. As I nuzzled him he fed me sweetmeats and fruits from his hand. Gently around my neck he placed a collar, light and with a brass nameplate inscribed upon the front,

Hamnet read it to me

"Mummer, Master Hamnet Shakespeare's Renowned Bear. None Should Do Him Harm. £10 reward if lost – come to Master Shakespeare at the Rose Theatre London."

Thus was I now much comforted. One of the men tied a sign to the outside of my cage, and Hamnet spoke to the men.

"Gentlemen, you know that I am here by kind permit of Mr. Henslowe and that my father is his ally and friend. Do thou such grace for me as to mind and care for this bear, for he is not vicious and knows not the wild and dreadful habits of some bears. He is here simply to be lodged and not baited. He will appear at the Rose Theatre upon the stage, mumming, as his name is Mummer."

The men murmured and laughed.

"Here is one shilling each for the five of thee," spoke Hamnet, and the men straightened up. "And you shall have this again for the week of this Mummer Bear's safekeeping. Let him not be afraid, fearful nor hurt."

The men doffed their caps, and said, "Nay sir, he shall be treated kindly."

"Master Hamnet sir," said one, "my name is Clem and I know well of thy renowned father, the playwright and showman. All here shall take a kind eye unto this bear and he shall be as well treated – yea better than – any bear here, like even unto the famous Sackerson." He gestured towards my neighbour, the huge bear in the solitary cage.

A group of yapping dogs sounded at the nearby wooden wall.

"Let not any dog nor man hurt him."

"Right – they shall not." Said Clem as the other men nodded.

* ** * *

I was stowed in a cage next to one containing several larger bears, many of them tired and wounded and angry. Some of them stared at me growling nastily. Among themselves they spoke and did mock me and my nameplate, my solitary cage and my clean fur, unlike theirs, which was matted. As night fell, I was restless in my cage, surrounded by, but apart from, the other bears. That night I could hear the fight at the bear-pit and was much frighted. I paced my cage and heard the anguished screams of the bears. l was upset by the smells of the frightened bears; I felt the bloodlust in the crowd and heard the screaming during the fight. But at last it stopped and there was cheering. In our cages there was many a loud snore and many a low and menacing growl as the bears started to wake and began pacing restlessly in their cages. Pacing back and forth in the cage next to mine was the bear of huge size which I had seen earlier. He looked as if he was from another age. I learned speedily that this was the great Sackerson, the most feared and famous fighting bear in all England.

He was pampered and well fed, his wounds were dressed, and, as he later told me, he was always withdrawn from his fights before he was badly hurt. Often the first few fierce hounds were soon replaced by others that were less valuable or fierce being thrown in for him to fight and bite, whilst the crowd bayed above and wagered sums of gold and silver upon him. Sackerson was a prized bear.

Now he woke all the bears up for a moonlight meeting. My cage was next to his and as I stared up at him, the mighty beast growled at me through the bars. He asked me who I was and if I had met any other bears. Then he said, "What are you doing here, my pampered young cub? You are too young to fight."

"But not too young to be eaten," growled another bear.

Some bears nodded and sniffed their agreement, for they all had seen me arrive, and how I had been placed in cage by myself and given sweetmeats. They saw my medallion and the ribbon about my neck and mocked me. "What sort of a noble are you?" Sackerson asked with a laugh and a deep growl. "Tell us of yourself ..."

I spoke thus, telling them the names Stander had told me in the forest: "Stander, Blind Robin, the mighty Sackerson, Ned of Canterbury or the great and giant bear Harry Hunks ..."

"Stander? What do you know of Stander?" interrupted Sackerson.

So I recounted my tale of the forest and all the bears stopped to listen. I told them about Stander, and all the bears pricked up their ears. "You've met Stander on the run! Whereabouts in a forest? How is he?" they chorused. But Sackerson said, "Wait. How do we know this young cub is telling the truth?" The old bear looked at me and demanded, "What else did Stander tell you?"

"About his mother and the wolves," I replied and told my tale of Stander and the frightful forest and all. Sackerson ordered the other bears to accept me, as he knew I was speaking truth about Stander.

Chapter 13
Sackerson's Story – and the Baiting

Upon my second night in the cage, the Friday, Sackerson spoke thus to me. The theatres were open but the bear-pits were closed to be cleaned and the bears rested for the dreaded Saturday night (which I feared I should come to soon enough.) The other bears mostly were asleep, their snoring a heave of growls and cries of pain as their dreams, like an oracle, foresaw the day that awaited their slumbers.

"Young Mummer. thou art a young bear and I am an old bear. Thou art small and I am very large," said Sackerson. "Thou art a gentle cub, and I am a renowned, fearsome, feared, most destructive and mighty bear. With great power I come, hotly like an earthquake, when the very ground and stone beneath me is torn asunder, and a storm of terrible thunder and lightning whirls about my claws and teeth and mighty muscle. I am a great bear. None other but myself has survived the baiting so long or is so huge and enormous in this our northern clime. Bears it is that reign supreme. This is why the men stage their great spectacles and their dreaded bloody shows about us. Not sheep nor horses do fight and leap like we do. I will tell thee of that which thou wilt never find in the history books – if thou wert able to read!

I shall tell unto thee a tale that hath never been told before of Warwickshire and the bears' great revolt.

"Three hundred years ago, in the village of Berming Ham, the home of Berm and his relatives, it was the night of the bears' revolt. The bears overcame their handlers and ran loose into the crowds of people. The hounds also ran wild in packs. Freed from fighting the dangerous bears, they turned upon the people. For days animals rampaged around the countryside. It was the hounds that were the worst, they did savage the sheep, bite the people and run in and out of their houses willy-nilly.

The bears mostly escaped into the forests, but many bears did attack sheep and cattle for they were most hungry, indeed starved.

"Whilst the populace had no swords, most of them were archers, for the King had bidden them go to the butts upon every Sunday afternoon to prepare one day to defend the realm. Thus did the yeomen of England become archers and in their houses would keep bows and arrows. It was with these weapons that the revolt was put down. Many bears escaped to the forests and hills, but thereafter many bears were hunted or captured for sport and no-one would tell the tale of Berming Ham and the night the bears revolted.

"This story has been passed down from captured bear to prisoner bear in the pits and squares and killing places. There is another animal that men bait and torture and that is the bull. Bull-baiting and bear-baiting go side by side.

"They say that there is a giant cat, the lion, that they call the King of the Beasts, for they are fierce in southern lands, where it is hot and there are no bears. But here in the northern lands we bears are supreme. After uncountable years we have conquered and defeated all other beasts. The mighty bear rules in the mountains and forests. No other creature is as heavy nor so well equipped with claws and teeth and mighty arms and a long reach, a rapid speed and a huge and towering bulk, or can stand or walk upon two legs as well as four!

"What creature grows so huge? Not the cow, nor the wolf. They say that in southern climes reigns the elephant. But no man has seen one here since the Romans left our island."

"How do you know?" I asked, mystified at Sackerson's great knowledge.

"Why, I have seen one in my dreams," he answered. "So you Mummer, you will grow large and need great feeding. Men keep not bears such as we – who eat five and twenty men's wages every day – without that they bait them or put them fighting for a bet against savage hounds, to earn their keep. So our show is false, trickery and fake. Only our blood is real.

"But a bear like myself, named and known, does well. When my master Henslowe puts me to fight, he makes a great display, first with fireworks, then jesters, jugglers, minstrels and clowns, with prancing horses and fire-eating fakirs.

"And amongst the men there are wager-makers who keep a book, like a merchant, sometimes written but more often in their heads, on which to bet, the bear or the hounds. Five packs of hounds do they line up against me, Mummer!"

"Five packs," I repeated. "How, great bear, shall you survive, even though you do thrive yet?"

"Mummer, thou should never know of this in thy reality, but here is how it happens. Pack after pack they release, and the hounds are all paraded first past the people. Then the other packs are led out of sight, and a young slavering pack is barked and yapped up against me. And they see me so they snarl and leap."

"I would be so frightened," I said.

"Yes, young Mummer, you would be, as indeed I am. In my heart I am gentle and, like thee, only wish to nuzzle and eat titbits, although I have grown fond of beer," continued Sackerson.

The night was all around us and the snores of the other bears had grown steady as Sackerson supped from his beer bucket and let me lick and sup a little therefrom also. "But sometimes the dogs have been fed a little so they are not so discontented as to wish to fight anything. Their mettle is no match for my skills! So I conquer the first four dogs with blows as they squeal away. Now the crowd is roaring! The torchlight shines around the Wooden O above us. The drunken crowds of people all around the bear-pit are roaring, screaming, gambling and drinking. But I the bear do not hear them. My eyes and ears are upon the next assault. At the gap between assaults from the packs I am given beer. My face is splashed with water and my arms rubbed down by the men. Now am I up again, a gladiator bear in the circus of the bear pit, the fighting arena. Now a new set of hounds comes towards me. These have not been fed and are angry and ready. I attack them in a whirl and one or two dogs limp away. Another is laid bloody before me, still heaving, with blood pouring out of its chest; another hound lies dead in the sawdust. The other dogs flee or cower, for they have been substituted, exchanged, replaced by Henslowe for the fine dogs that were paraded before the show started. I am Sackerson and must thrive. And it is upon me that the offers of money are wagered that the dogs shall beat me. A man can receive thrice three golden ducats for one Pound if I lose.

"Thus do the humans (if Henslowe deserves the name of human!) look after me. Thus thrive I. After the fights am I long rested and well fed, rubbed down, taken out sometimes in a great muzzle so that people can pay a penny to hold me by the chain. I heard one man say with pride: 'I have held Sackerson by the chain twenty times.'"

And Sackerson finished talking, but that night I slept not one wink. I lay shivering from fright as the bears began to howl a great cacophony of pain, a symphony of hurt. Nearby, beyond the wooden wall, the dogs barked and yapped and snarled, shouting outright for the bears they meant to hurt in the next day's sport. The great bear Sackerson eyed me silently from his cage. He had observed the special treatment that I had received, with much water and fruit, when the men bantered with me next to my cage. I had been much pleased to have this company but now the men had long gone to their beds, while the miseries and cries of the enchained beasts shattered my very soul. Several bears were swaying their heads from side to side in the darkness of their cages. Most of the torches were out, with only one or two flickering fresh high upon the walls. The smell in these filthy chambers was dreadful – there was sweat and sickness, pain and fear. The place was very frightening and I freely wept as I lay upon my floor on the straw and wept for my lost Hamnet and my life of joy – my vanished summer's lease of happiness.

I recalled Stander telling me that there was no promise that a man could give to a bear except pain.

** *

That night, after the fireworks, the baiting began. The men came into the chamber and unlocked a huge bear. He was much scarred, and swayed as he walked. I saw and smelt as they gave him a bucket of beer. He swilled his head into it and drank greedily therefrom. Then, upon a heavy chain, he was taken out from our sight up into the arena.

My cage was next to the wooden walls of the bear pit and I could now see through the plank work, with my eye pressed against a crack. So I could witness as the show of evil unfolded before me. With steel did they chain this solitary bear, Orso, to a great wooden stake driven deep into the ground. Into the arena, on leashes held by men, then bounded a snarling slavering pack of huge hungry hounds. There was a great roar from the crowd as the pack were brought in, barking and snapping and straining, feverish at the leashes that held them.

65

Orso the bear drew himself up to his full height and vainly tugged upon the chain that held him. The crowd above, drunken and noisy, was roaring, screaming, and shouting as they wagered upon their favourite, be it the bear or the hounds. "Orso, Orso, I'll wager five Pounds," called one. Then unleashed, one by one, the hounds leapt toward the bear. Several great and fierce beasts were slavering and snarling at the poor bear and lunging at him, so that his face and paws and neck bled. He fell but I could not endure to see any more. I fell back into a corner of the cage and wrapped my paws around my head . Later I heard that a bear had died, but I shall never know if it was Orso.

The other big bears became anxious at this. Some of them were too sick to fight that night. They all wondered who would be picked next. There was much growling and I watched as the great dark bear Sackerson was chosen. Beer was brought to him and he drank it from a jug held for him. Later he returned, safe and sound, with little sign of the ordeal he had just experienced.

The fireworks had gone off, and the crowds had left.

Hamnet was asleep somewhere in the city but all I knew was that I was alone and without him for the first time in my memory since the dark woods had frighted my soul, for bears do have souls.

*** *

I opened my eyes. The screams and cries from the bear pits had died down. Many bears were sleeping fitfully ,whimpering and occasionally lashing out and growling in their troubled slumber. I was aware of the huge dark shape of the mighty Sackerson in the next cage. He growled to me, "Come to the corner, Mummer." I obeyed and moved near to the corner of my cage, and then perceived that Sackerson's mighty paws were squeezed around the iron bar of my living tomb. I deemed that the great bear, the most renowned fighting bear, the most feared baiting bear in all of England, one day even to be mentioned in dear Master Shakespeare's play, was helping me escape.

"Don't just stand there," growled Sackerson, "Help. Pull! Pull!" he wheezed.

I wrapped my small paws around the iron bar and pulled with all my might. Slowly the huge bar bent more and more, and then suddenly there was a loud crack which awakened many bears. Sackerson and I

66

in our adjoining space behind the bars fell over as the iron bar came completely out of its stone base. We set our paws around the bar, whilst bears in the cages around us fell back into their unquiet slumber. Then Sackerson moved round and, hunching his great shoulders, he pushed the bar so that it moved clear. "Come in here," he growled. I squeezed around the broken bar of iron, and edged into Sackerson's cage. It smelt of bear and beer. In the corner was a great wooden bucket of fresh ale, the fine scent of which was a cloud of wonder to my senses.

"Come here cub, that I might see thee take a drink to fortify thyself."

I put my head into the strange sweet smelling bucket and the fumes enveloped my nose. I drank deeply until Sackerson grabbed my arm and pulled me out.

"Enough! 'Tis to fortify thyself, not for thee to become a sot that I give thee drink. Now climb unto me and look up atop to this corner of the roof." He gestured to where there was a glimmer of moonlight. "That plank is loosened, Mummer. Do thou push it and go beyond to the wall. Watch thyself, for the wall is high. Here in London we are much mured about with high stone walls and iron cages. We bears are English, natural born, yet we are prisoners."

Sackerson held my leg in his great paw. "Now climb unto me and up into this corner of the roof." I clambered up on his shoulder. Standing there I stretched out and seized the edge of the roof, from whence a light breeze came. I pushed myself through and was out upon the roof of the Paris Gardens bear-pits. I crawled carefully from the top of the roof to the wall. Along it I could see the backstage area of the Rose Theatre. I could hear voices and music but it was the smell of the theatre – the greasepaint – that moved me on. I could almost smell Hamnet. I clambered down from the wall and then across the garden into the theatre itself. I looked for Hamnet.

And there he was! My arrival had interrupted a rehearsal. Hamnet cried out happily as he saw me. When I leapt up onto the stage, all the actors and all the stagehands ran off at the other side. The stage was empty save for Hamnet and me. "Excellent! Perfect! Wonderful! Give that goodly bear an apple!" cried Master Shakespeare. "That's how to clear the stage. *Exit pursued by a bear!*"

67

"Surely," said Mr. Babbage, the renowned actor who was watching the rehearsals, "a player in a costume would be safer, Will?"

"There's no point having a man in costume," said Master Shakespeare, "People see real bears every day here."

"Can it be a real bear, Father? can it be Mummer?" pleaded Hamnet.

And thus it was that I found my way once again into the theatre, wherein I performed many tricks, some indeed unbidden, such as swirling a cape and wooden sword, wearing Caesar's wreath and toga, holding my paw forth and growling a great declamation, or dancing to an eastern tune with graceful steps.

Chapter 14
Summer 1595 at The Old Moor's House

When the residence for the Shakespeare family at the Old Moor's House was ready for our party, I was soon liberated from my nightmare existence among the bears. At dawn that day our long train of wagons, horses, men and carriers wound along the curve of Old Father Thames. Across the river the bright shadows of the Tower of London were gleaming white against the   blue and sunny sky. We were swept through the gates, held open by lackeys, of a strange and splendid residence, white with curved walls, narrow windows and a minaret. We went through a Moorish arch into a pleasant shaded courtyard, cool in the midst of the summer's heat. A fountain played in the courtyard and I looked out, through the wooden and steel bars of my cage, for Hamnet, but to no avail – until at last he appeared with his father. Master Shakespeare was to reside with his entourage here at the Old Moor's house, which would be his London dwelling.

A voice resounded: " The Moor's House! Nay, more of a Palace, hey Master Will! And a good time of day unto you all." We turned to see from whence came this buoyant greeting. It was Master Philip Henslowe. Much to my surprise he patted my head gently and fed some grapes and sweet fruit to me. Never has a bear escaped from me before," he muttered, no doubt thinking of my burst to freedom from his vile cages, when I had arrived on the stage of the Rose theatre. He and Master Will moved away talking together, and Hamnet and I started to explore our new kingdom – our realm, our empire.

Next to the walls was a new built large timber-clad hall, rising above vaulted arches of brick. I smelt the fishes and saw the river gleaming beyond, the water lapping on to the building. Two decorated boats bobbed up and down, resting and then again moving as the morning tide flooded in. I watched now as Master Will and Hamnet bounded up the stone staircase to the upper floor above the arches where the hall had been gilded; the workmen were still putting the finishing touches on it.

"We shall live here in these upper quarters," said Master Will to Hamnet. "And here we shall find every need provided – food for our minds and our bellies. Thou art in Southbank London, wherein men have trod and traded since the Romans came to this fair land. As for our labours, our great endeavour, our purpose … We are but a half mile from the Rose Theatre. Master Henslowe is undertaking great renovations there before our shows begin."

Hamnet began throwing me fruit from his father's table, which I caught in my paws. "Well," said Mr Henslowe, "He certainly is a clever bear. And no bear has ever escaped from me before," he repeated as if still astonished. "Save one, renowned Stander and that was from a cart. How this young cub got out from Paris Gardens is a mystery." Henslowe scratched his head.

Hamnet said, "Dear Father I am worried that Master Henslowe will return Mummer to the bear-pits. He will not survive those pits, he is like to die of fright."

His father replied, "There is no need to fright the bear with a return to the baiting pits. He can and shall live here in this courtyard. It is gated for our better protection, and he will be safe. Many of our young actors and stage men shall live here at the house, and Master Henslowe will charge that each man hath food – a meal each evening, be he builder or carpenter or actor."

"Or indeed the bear's good counsel and manager," remarked Hamnet about himself, to general laughter.

Outside, the street was all a-bustle with smells and cries, and soon Master Greenaway's men had hauled up the bedding, the furniture and the drapes. Two housekeeping ladies jollied about, opening the windows and laying out the covers upon the beds. We all stood and looked out as the windows were opened. There before and below us stretched the river. Bright sunlight flowed in and beyond the river we saw the skyline of London. "Thus shall our fortunes be made," cried Master Henslowe, his voice loud with wine. "Indeed there will be new theatre walls at the Rose. The new plays will be greater, and the Lord Chamberlain's men shall perform. And thou, Master Will, not a mere substitute, subordinate vector bailiff or secretary, but as Theatre

Master, Owner and Captain, will lead the profit to our venture. Ye shall be a sharer!"

"Shout not so loudly, Master Philip, in thy cups," said Master Will. "For pitchers have ears, and revenue men prowl the land. We still pay for the Armada threat, as I am sure thou knowest. Let us not talk of such matters here this day. All I say unto thee is to keep my name out of thy book of accounts," he said. "Write not me down either as writer or actor or owner or dreamer or bearmaster!"

They laughed. "Thou shalt keep the books," said Master Henslowe, but Master Shakespeare replied, "And I say that thou shalt, and good books will they be. But nowhere in thy scribblings, Henslowe, needst thou attribute one penny piece to me as in my own person," said Master Shakespeare, "Else by such it should be misconstrued that I owe or am due to pay some other money in tax! Say not that I did receive on such and such a date for such and such a performance."

"Let the coin be the contract," said Master Henslowe, taking from his pocket a fat golden Pound coin which glinted in the sunlight.

"Why, Master Henslowe," he began, paused, being now, like his companion, somewhat drunk upon the fine French brandy which was passing between them. "Show me where it says William Shakespeare on that gold coin." He waved the coin, which gleamed in the firelight, while the ladies moved around them with fresh jugs and plates of bread.

"It does not."

"Nor doth it say nor reveal it is Henslowe's gold piece. Yea the coin is the contract, the coin is anonymous. Such is the silent power of riches. Thy takings at the theatre from the audiences of groundlings swell thy fat purses of coin."

They both took another drink but now from the well, and Henslowe lowered his voice. "The Queen's grandfather, Henry the Seventh of that name, did strike fear into men's hearts with his sequestering and plundering, his predatory despoiling of the nobility and the merchants by false transactions. Henry the Eighth, the Queen's father, ended that – his blessed daughter, our Sovereign Lady Queen Elizabeth, the First of that name ..."

"The First of that name," said Master Shakespeare, raising his chalice of wine, "doth seek more modern ways to raise her coin, by those horned devils – taxes! So be glad that it says not that Master

71

Shakespeare owneth this gold struck coin. And let it leave no trail behind thee of jealous writings in that work of book of yours, Henslowe!"

He rattled the leather-bound book of accounts that fell from Henslowe's inner pockets.

Chapter 15
Bad Bear and Good Bear!

And so Hamnet came back again with me, his bear, to the Old Moor's house. Together with Mr. Henslowe's two sons, Henry and Richard, Hamnet was to be tutored at this riverside house and garden which his father Master Shakespeare was renting. While I was listening to the two men talking, I had dropped off to sleep and was dreaming that I was in the forest amid the chill snow, at the edge of a frozen lake. In my dream I saw what at first I thought were white-covered bushes moving in the wind, and then methought I could smell wolves! It seemed to me that their heads had turned at me and looked in my direction with hungry and covetous eyes and I began to tremble. I woke up in a sweat but shivering at the same time, even though it was the heat of high summer of the year 1595.

At the Old Moor's House, Hamnet and I had most spacious chambers upon the upper floor. The windows had all been barred and the wooden door had been replaced by one made stronger with an iron bar. In the corner was my own special den of leather and wood, enclosed like a kennel for hounds, but larger. There none could harm me or touch me or see me whilst I slept. Save for Tham Greenaway, Master Will and Master Hamnet, none came in there. There I had my iron bowls of fruit and food. Sometimes, slipping a chain about my neck and with the door well locked, Hamnet would lead me out onto the balcony and down the broad staircase through a gate and on to the riverside wharf, where I could bathe.

But one day, after Hamnet had returned me to our quarters and taken off the chain, his father called him most urgently downstairs. So he left me alone. I prowled around the room and soon I discovered that Hamnet had failed to bar the door. It was a warm day and I wanted to go back to the cooling water of the river, so I went down the staircase by myself to the riverside. Back in the water I was happy, splashing my fur. Then the sun went in and I thought to go back to my warm quarters. Alas, when I reached the gate to the stairs, it was secured. I could not go back! Where could I go?

73

I wandered along the river bank, and soon found myself in a marvelous place, where there were amazing stalls with delicious smelling fruits, which I could not forbear but to eat. I looked at the people who were at the stalls, to see if they were angry that I was eating their fruits, but they fled , with much shouting, they did not stay with me. I sat down in the middle of the marketplace and soon there was no-one else there, all having run away except for a youth who came gently toward me ,fed me fruit and made friends with me. He told me he was called Ali and had run away from his Turkish master. He told me how his master too once owned a bear, and how he and the bear had been friends because they both had to serve the master. He sat down by me so that I felt less alone.

I think I slept for a while. Then suddenly I awoke and heard the voice of Hamnet calling "Mummer!" And there he was, with his father, and holding my chain. A crowd of people moved nervously behind them.

I gladly submitted to wear the chain and Hamnet led me home, reproaching me for frightening all the people in the market. Hamnet told me how he had gone downstairs when his father had called him, to tell him about the performance at the Rose theatre. Then he had come up again and found I was not there. There had followed what seemed to them to be many agonizing hours, whilst the stagehands and men of the actors' company were asked, for a shilling each, and upon the promise of a reward, to look for the bear. I was told by Hamnet that many of them spent but a little time searching but then went to the ale house known as the Black Bear to spend their shilling. But Hamnet found me for he never ceased searching. And Ali became a good friend to Hamnet for he warned him that the Town Watch had been summoned and would come to the Old Moor's House to look for me. So when they arrived, not long after we had returned home, Master Shakespeare was ready for them. The next morning they were up before the magistrates where Master William paid the modest fine. Hamnet told me that his father had sweetly bribed the Clerk and a pamphleteer to write no more upon it.

Ali was given a job helping at the Rose and tending to me for Hamnet. He was very caring and kind to me. Hamnet later went to the market and paid some coin to those whose goods I had purloined

The news that Master Shakespeare had told Hamnet when he had summoned him downstairs, and I, a bad bear, had gone down to the water, was that there was to be a performance of the play of Richard the Third at the Rose Theatre in no more than two weeks time – and that the Queen herself might grace us with her presence.

We were in the Yard a day or so later, when Master Hamnet was called over to the gate, and upon walking outside was surrounded by men, and shouting for help. I saw him struggle and then he was carried off by them!

I could do nothing for I was in my cage. I growled and howled for I sensed something was very wrong and could hear Hamnet's cries

Tham swiftly brought Hamnet's father into the yard and spoke with him

"They was rough looking men, Master Shakespeare." Said Tham. William Shakespeare ran quickly down the outside staircase, followed by Henslowe, who called past him to his men. "Aye and they was rough mannered too," added Ned. He was sitting on the floor whilst Mary from the inn dabbed at his bleeding headwound.

"We weren't far away. From the corner of my eye I saw them walk toward the bear, looking at him as folk do, sir. Young Master Hamnet had just closed the Beare's cage sir, for the night after he had walked him to and fro in the yard. We thought nothing of them sir. They walked past the gate of the yard. One was leading two horses and the other two came into the yard and made as if to look at the bear. "

They all looked at me and nodded.

Ned Continued" Mr Henslowe had been stood apart talking to his men, and when they thought we wasn't looking, two of them grabbed Master Hamnet who had walked to the gate. I yelled at them and as I moved towards the man in front of me, he smashed the cudgel on my head and smote me mightily."

"And they have seized Master Hamnet. They dragged him away when they fled," said Tham.

Master Shakespeare called out, '"Long Harry, do you and some men stay here at the Moor's house to guard it, in case this is some ploy to leave it empty while we all chase after Hamnet."

Several men of the theatre company had woken by then and filled the courtyard, some carrying stout sticks and others holding flaming

75

torches aloft. "Unlock and Bring the bear, Tham," commanded Master Shakespeare. It is not three minutes since they took the boy. We must follow hotly upon the chase. The bear hath a great nose and shall like a finer hound lead us to Hamnet."

I had been pacing furiously back and forth in my cage and growling mightily. I had seen what had happened. The men had dragged Hamnet, cuffing his mouth. They had flung him across one of their horses.

Barely had Tham unlocked me from my cage and put a chain about me than I did run toward the gate, and, sniffing the air, ran in the direction the men had taken Hamnet.

Now free with Tham holding my light chain I ran into the night

The dark smell of the horses, scared by what had happened, still lingered. Then I roared. The streets were not empty. There were still groups of folk staggering from the pubs and bawdy houses. We stumbled on into darkened streets, the houses shuttered and stable yards dark. At the end of one street I could smell the river … and the horses! Now we turned and the horse odor was strong, Tham and another man held me as I battered at the gate to the wharf. It was closed with a great chain and impassable, but soon our men had removed the chain. There were the horses, tied to a rail. The warehouse wall was in great disrepair, the roof open to the night. Still deeper in and darker now, we slowed our pace, but I could still smell Hamnet. We passed through ruined buildings until we came out upon the edge of the water – and there was Hamnet, shouting and struggling as the men tried to force him onto a barge with a drooping sail although the wind was up. Hamnet cried out, and I rolled and roared, while all the men ran forward. I strained with them, and then Tham dropped my chain and I raced toward Hamnet.

A great blow fell unto me as one of the men struck me with a club. I roared and snarled and then leapt toward the ruffian in an angry mood. He soon became the first human I had ever deeply bitten! Soon we had overcome them. Some of them managed to run away, hotly chased by Henslowe's men, but two of them were caught and questioned. I heard them claim that it was a plot to seize Hamnet and hold him for ransom. These men were led away by Henslowe's men and we never saw them again. One day much later, Henslowe said to Hamnet, "Fear those men no more, for they are both let blood and now slumber in Neptune's deep kingdom."

After Hamnet's return he cuddled me as we listened to Mr. Henslowe and Master Will musing over Hamnet's kidnapping.

"If it happened not for ransom, for I cannot truly believe those men's confessions "said Henslowe "then it were pressing"
"What means thou by pressing " Hamnet asked
Henslowe replied to him
"Tis said that there are press gangs which seek to abduct pretty and talented lads to be either Choristers or to Act in some lewd Theatre for men. This comes from Her Majesty issuing warrants that men and boys may be press ganged, either for Choirs, the Navy or other services. There are some men who do misuse these warrants and capture boys to be held in A covert Theatre to preform"
But that is true evil" cried Shakespeare
'Tis so but tis rife in our land"said Henslowe
"Well none shall do that in our Theatre" said Master Will
"Let each boy be apprenticed not to the theatre but to an individual player, an actor who can mentor the boys and teach them the craft of Theatre"
This much shall we do at the Rose."

Chapter 16

We are to play before the Queen

The Old Moor's House was alive with the news that Master William Shakespeare was to stage his political play, about King Richard, the Third of that name, for the Queen. I knew this play well and indeed had mimed and mummed alongside Hamnet at many an InnYard around Stratford for silver coin.

When Hamnet held aloft on a parchment the speech of King Richard, he would declaim in a most vociferous and loud mode of speech: "The unlicked bear whelp that knoweth no impression like the dam." As he spake it, I was there, hunching my back as Hamnet had taught me. Bending forward whilst remaining hunched of back, I would strut to and fro, a silk cloth upon my shoulder like unto a light jerkin, with the sign of the Hog, King Richard's own sign, upon the waist, back and sleeve.

Upon my head Hamnet had fixed a bright shiny crown by means of a secret strap. The crown had shone bright in the lanterns and torchlight illumination of the courtyards of the country inns where we had performed before we had come to London. Now Master Will was going to allow us to strut on the stage at the Rose Theatre in the late afternoon. Our show would serve to amuse and warm up the audience as a comic preparation for the tragedy that would follow .

Hamnet had explained to me that Robert Cecil, the Queen's Intelligencer, had commanded Master Shakespeare and the Queen's Men to perform the tragedy of Richard the Third in such a way as to stress the monstrous character unto which the previous dynasty had descended. He wanted all men to mark how much better for the protection of this land had been the Tudor rulers, her Majesty's father and grandfather. Master Cecil made sure that the audience would understand the virtues, the right and entitlement of our Lady Queen Elizabeth to be seated upon the throne of this mighty nation. And for her right, our navies had nobly saved Britannia. He wanted the audience to remember how even the wind from heavens had served her majesty when the might of Spain had dared to plan to assault this island with the Armada. Thus the ships had been driven round these isles in storms, their hopes being dashed on Irish shores. So Hamnet did recount to me, from the tales his father had told him. These tales were told to the audience at the Rose, and were to be told to the Queen at her palace at Greenwich.

For our prelude to the play, Hamnet had shown me how to draw one paw awkwardly toward my chest and hold it there as if crippled, whilst I would stride about the stage and he would read in a clear voice: "If I cannot prove the lover, I'll play the villain." At this I would let loose a roar, a loud violent growl, to fright the very souls of the audience, the cublings and groundlings who had paid their pennies to be there loved me and did laugh and applaud vigorously.

Oftimes did we rehearse this scene.

***

It was a Saturday – the Saturday, a few days before Master Shakespeare's company were to perform before Queen Elizabeth. Before the tragedy of Richard the Third, Hamnet and I were to entertain the Queen. His father had specified it so, and it was announced: "Master Hamnet Shakespeare and his good and true friend the renowned Bear, Mummer, aptly named for his great miming to Master William Shakespeare's three soliloquys, and now as familiar a name as Sackerson or Blind Ned or Harry Hunks, will perform before the Queen and a noble audience."

And Master Shakespeare wrote thus, unto his dear wife Anne, and his daughters Judith and Susannah, as Hamnet read it to me:

Mummer will perform one of his special mimes, that of Mark Anthony's lament of Julius Caesar, which I have but now penned for a future play. Mummer will strut with a toga over his shoulders and draped over his arm, and whilst Hamnet reads, he will make gestures. When Hamnet reads "Lend me your ears", he will touch both ears with both paws at which the toga will fall down, we hope to much laughter. Then Hamnet will step forward and redrape the toga. Mummer will wear a laurel wreath. After that, Mummer will put himself into a hunched form, to become Richard the Third. Thus hunched, he will growl and prance whilst Hamnet reads the soliloquy of the hunchback king.

All is well for our preparations. I shall write more soon. My heart is with thee all, my beautiful and dutiful family.

WS

From dawn by the misty hot river known as Old Father Thames, a slow pale sunlight came over us. Hamnet led me gently to the courtyard of the Old Moor's House, wherein we shared a bedroom. All was a bustle, men were carrying great pieces of cloth and wood, for that was the day when the special mirthful comic shows would delight her Majesty and then the populace. Hamnet led me upon a light chain, for my comfort more than for any security, and to it was attached, in silver and brass, a plaque proclaiming me: "Mummer: the Actor Bear, property of Master Hamnet Shakespeare, The Rose Theatre, Bankside, £20 Reward for this Bear's safe return if he should be lost."

A year's wages for my safe return! It is true that I had sometimes in my wild and cumbersome adventurous days run away, but I was resolved to do so no more. Then Hamnet paused by the open cage door, and put upon me a light muzzle made of pure silver but blackened for its purpose. My muzzle – but only Hamnet and I knew the big secret of this muzzle and why I was to wear it upon special occasions.

Then we embarked into the polished oak and iron travelling cage, with leather hood and curtains, now all open. It was especially made for me by Stratford-upon-Avon's skilled craftsmen. The scents of the morning flooded my nose, so much more sensitive than the noses of humans. The spectators would see in me an English bear, a rare creature. It was told among bears how most of our ancestors in this fair country had long been slaughtered or baited or hunted to death, just for the pleasure of men. England, nay indeed Europe, had seen much cruelty to my breed, and in these days the setting of packs of hounds upon chained bears had become a sport much encouraged. Those bears living in England were mostly from distant lands like Russia. Many of them resided in Southbank, London, where was I once, at the infamous bear baiting pits, though others lived at other bull and bear baiting rings across the realm of England. And Queen Elizabeth was the most avid enjoyer of the sport of bear baiting!

I could smell the opening of the stables and see the horses being backed out for their morning watering. as the steam rose from the courtyard. "This will be a hot day, Mummer!" said Hamnet to me, "in more ways than one. Soon we are to appear before her dread Majesty our Sovereign Queen Elizabeth, the first of that name, vanquisher of the Armada, Saviour of England and Protector of the Church of England. Yet there remain great dangers to her from the Spaniards."

I listened to this tale, my head deep in a bucket of water, my second of that day, from which I drank. Elizabeth! I feared as I heard that dread name. Did Hamnet not understand that the Queen might want me baited, and order Hamnet or Master Shakespeare to accomplish this? Would they dare to disobey a command from the Queen? I shook these thoughts from my bearish mind. I was still young in years, and the smell of the berries which Hamnet held for me was stronger in my mind than the fearful memories of Paris Gardens. I felt no fear in this my travelling home – no cruelties would seep their way in. Hamnet and Mr. Shakespeare's men all knew me well. Like Hamnet the men loved me well, and did feed and pet me. Sometimes when my dear Hamnet was not aware, they would even give me beer to sip. They were staunch men, loyal to the Shakespeares, and honest. All of them, it seemed, worked in the theatre. The young lads would dress as women for the stage, since the law announced that true women were not to appear on stage – thus was then the strangeness of human ways. Hamnet had taught me to be cautious, but I knew I was safe with the family and the actors with whom I played. I knew no angry moments.

Hamnet spoke to me before we left, "'Tis good for you Mummer that you know well where thy easement place is in thy cage. It is for your every grace and comfort that we do care for thee, Mummer." He patted the square box in a trench at the back of the cage wherein I might ease myself. I knew that Hamnet and his father kept *another* box under the planking, beneath my house of easement, wherein they had a sealed iron casket. It contained Master Shakespeare's movables, coins of silver and gold, and diamonds from Antwerp which Mr. Cecil had given Master Henslowe for some secret use. So I was Lord Protector of the Treasury also, whilst Tham Greenaway was my groom and guardian, commanded by my captain, Hamnet, to wash and clean me and place fresh straw in my cage.

That summer at the Rose Theatre had we performed many times.

Hamnet would lead me through the streets all alive with hawkers and butchers and people crying out their wares, and many would gape at us as we passed. That summer had flown by in the heat and crowds of Southwark. Then we learned that we were not to perform before the Queen at the Rose, but instead to travel to appear before her at

81

Greenwich Palace, where the air and situation were more to Her Majesty's liking.

Great preparations were made for the day. These entailed us travelling by barge along the river. Whilst we were departing, Hamnet was hugging me tightly, I heard him tell Tham of his fears about our visit to the Queen. He was sitting half in the cage, with his legs dangling out as we were wheeled gently around upon our wagon to where we were joined to the horses. "Yea, there are rumours of a plot to kill her. There are always plots, many have been spoken thereof. But I hear that a Spaniard will come secretly, supported by certain high born nobles, and that he will be allowed near unto her to strike."

"She is well guarded, is she not?" asked Tham

"Aye, but this plot is well planned they say, and much thought upon by those who desire a change of monarch. And it could happen, I surmise, at one of the queen's entertainments at Greenwich, at a time where she is known to be in one place and all eyes are upon the show." Said Hamnet

"It may be a pistol then?"

"Aye, a musket is the feared danger, I heard Lord Cecil tell as much to my father, and all now are searched who come into her presence. But on a day when many nobles or ambassadors may be there, the guards may not prove so cautious. Lord Cecil told my father that they must be obliged to put themselves or their agents near unto the plotters' circle and learn their plans and prevent tragedy from occurring."

"Who shall do this?"

" My Father has spoken unto Master Henslowe that he and his minions may have a care to learn such intelligence as he can .

Hamnet spoke then to me, "Today you will join a mirthful comic show, to be held at the great audience room at the Palace of Greenwich, a Palace which the Queen likes for her summer residence because of the delightfulness of its situation," as she has said. "Today and tomorrow there is to be a special festival. Tomorrow, Mummer, shalt thou appear before the Queen herself. There is to be a magnificent pageant at the Palace and upon the river, with decorated vessels, a muster of London's men-at-arms in historic clothing, a flamboyant and magnificent water pageant with a mock great castle being attacked by ships, and then fireworks and a great celebratory parade of captured Spanish treasure following the Spanish Armada. These are amongst the lavish displays which will take place upon the River Thames and in the grounds of Greenwich Palace which fronts the water. And this very morning, tomorrow being the first day of this feast thereof, we are to travel with our wagon and horses, down to the dockside nearby and all to be loaded for Greenwich upon Mr. Henslowe's barge, together with many other pieces and entertainments. Mr. Banks and his horse Morocco will sail with us. A voyage of stellar and renowned performers! And you, master Mummer, and I, Sir Hamnet the Magnificent, are to appear early, to warm her Majesty's ardour where she and many nobles will sit in the Great Audience Chamber. Thou and I will appear on stage before her and we will open the tragedy with a great and amusing comic show!"

While much that he said was beyond my bearish understanding, in a manner I comprehended it all, for there was a great sense almost like to thunder and lightning in his manner and speech. We shared our excitement and were ready to make at last a performance that would delight the Queen.

We travelled in the barge, and at last we docked at Greenwich Palace. Enthroned in my travelling cage, I was slowly moved around to the stables, astern of the Palace, from where the horses were released, for we were to stay the night there. But tonight we made all preparation and brooked no delay, for tomorrow was to be a busy day. Soon we were to enter Greenwich Palace to perform before the Queen!

* * *

Our great and fearful day was to be tomorrow. Hamnet was trembling with excitement. To perform here at Greenwich Palace, before Her Majesty and her distinguished guests, the Duke of Hapsburg and other notables! In the garden, whilst the guests were to be seated in the great hall, there were comic shows and mirthful entertainments to be held, duly orchestrated by Philip Henslowe. I had heard him say to Master Shakespeare that he yearned for a knighthood – although he was rich and powerful, he was not born a nobleman but was a wondrous showman.

This day there was to be no baiting, but only a celebration of the Queen's birthday. There were to be fireworks, some jesters, jugglers,

83

and dancing and masques and some enactments from Master Shakespeare's play *The True History of King Richard the Third*. It was told to the audience that the play had been completed and published in 1594 but not played by cause of the theatres being closed for fear of the plague.

The Lord Chamberlain had come to view the preparations and ensure to all was fit for the Queen, especially in the matter of the legitimacy of her reign, that it should not be sullied by her being present at any lewd event. And Sir Robert Cecil was there, the man known as Elizabeth's spymaster general. As always his concern was the security of the Queen. This hunchbacked man, the son of Lord Burghley, was effectively Master of England.

As I dwelt in my cage by Greenwich Palace that night ,I could smell the river and the fruitful and foul smells and stenches from the river and stables , but I nuzzled deeper into the berry bag Hamnet had left me and filled myself therefrom. Then did I lay down and dream, my mind going back to my time with Stander in the great Forest and how freely we ran through the trees and the cornfields. At once we were chasing sheep though in my dream they outran us, Stander was purring his deep growl ...

But suddenly I was awake. It was past midnight at Greenwich palace and I smelt strangers in the stables.. There were men near my cage, the dank sour smell of men that seemed not to have washed in days. I felt about me something akin to the fright of the bear-pits. Quietly I opened my eyes. Two men were standing at the end of my cage, speaking in whispers. The fur rose upon the back of my neck. It seemed to me that they were hiding and talking too quietly. One passed an object to the other and as he did, it touched my cage and there was a metallic sound. It glinted as it passed from one man to the other. I gave a deep snarl and sat up. The two men were startled and moved sharply a few paces away from the cage, but I could still hear them. My eyes revealed to me that one of them was short and stout and the other, the one who smelt so bad, was much taller and thinner.

The first man said, "There I am done, my promise to the Ambassador is fulfilled. Use it well, my Spanish friend! May God be with you and may there soon be a King of Spain upon the English throne."

"Commend me to his Majesty," said the taller man and then the shorter man was gone.

The tall thin man stood there looking at me. I could see him better as my eyes adjusted to the dark. His face was in shadows, and he wore dark clothes – a cloak and a black hat with a broad brim. I growled at him. He moved closer. He banged the cage again with some metal, a blade that I now could see that he held in his hand. He laughed harshly as I started a false lunge toward him, growling. But then he was gone.

Chapter 17
I meet Her Majesty

I was full of a mighty fear as we came into the presence of the Queen. My nose and my fright the night before had alerted me to what turned out to be a great and dangerous event, one in which I took a leading role, even though I had no script for it beforehand as I had for King Richard.

Before the play itself, we were due to perform our comedy, in which I was to be King Richard while Hamnet would recite the words.

We settled upon the low stage and slowly the audience quieted and in came a glittering figure who took her place on the highest chair in the middle of the audience,it was Her Majesty Queen Elizabeth!

Master Shakespeare was not with us because he was urging upon the actors in the play proper about the importance of them being ready with their parts. But Hamnet was with me when the madness and danger happened and I shall use the words he later spake to his father – I was the central character in the scene, but I could not use human words to tell Master William Shakespeare what had passed just a few moments earlier.

After it all

Hamnet stood before his Father and said:

"Dear Father, what great alarums have we witnessed this day! Cecil himself came, I remembered him from his visit to our dwelling in Stratford. 'And is that bear muzzled?' asked the Lord Chamberlain of me, and I answered, 'Oh yes, at all times and he is a most safe and placid bear, I swear, for it has always been the case. I have brought him up with love from a cub and he has never known anger nor cruelty nor baiting.'"

Then Hamnet became agitated in telling his tale, and Master Shakespeare spoke to him, "Calm, my son, I see that thou hast been crying and there is blood upon thy sleeve."

"'Tis not mine father, but the man's."

"What man? Speak on my son and tell thy tale."

"We were standing there, ready to start our performance, and it was then that Mummer did the strangest thing, Father, something he hath never done before. First he sniffed deeply and stared out at the audience. Then the brave bear ripped at the back of the muzzle which I was just affixing before the performance to the Queen. Then Mummer, broke free of me, knocked me over and lunged, roaring and growling, straight at the Queen who was seated in front of us

. I ran after him as the bear leapt of the stage and appeared to lunge toward the Queen!. All had frozen like unto a tableau, Father. I could not reach Mummer. And when he was a few feet away from Her Majesty, Mummer leapt towards her. I was speechless, no-one in the room had moved and all eyes were upon us when this man appeared. He was an assassin, a tall man in a cloak who burst through the drapes behind the Queen. Mummer jumped toward him and there was a loud gunshot as Mummer leapt upon the stranger, and roaring and biting pushed him down upon the floor behind the Queen and growling he pinned him to the ground.

I cried out but Mummer heard me not! And guards with pikes and lances moved toward Mummer as if to injure him and I flung myself in front of where Mummer and the man were wrestling on the ground. Mummer stood up and moved away from the man, I rushed forward and just prevented a guard from piercing Mummer with a pike, for many were confused and had not realised what had happened. Some thought that the would-be assassin was Mummer himself, and one of the Queen's guards was trying to shoot Mummer to prevent him injuring the Queen! All was great confusion and chaos. Then Sir Robert Cecil spoke, 'The bear hath saved the queen. Master Shakespeare's bear hath saved the Queen's life!' There was a great cheer from the party of nobles and soldiers and all the assembly.

"The Queen leant round to look at the bear and me, as I was now fixing the muzzle to Mummer. He was now placid, though somewhat trembling from his desperate exertions. The Queen demanded, 'Come hither, boy. What is thy name?' I replied, 'Hamnet Shakespeare, ma'am.' 'You are the son of Master William Shakespeare, our fine playwright and actor,' said the monarch, and I told her I was. 'We have spoken with thy father already,' she added, and paused, deep in thought. Then she continued, 'And this bear, is he a baiting bear?'

"'Oh no, Ma'am,' I told the Queen. 'His name is Mummer, he is sweet and gentle and hath been mine for a long time, since he was a small unlicked cub. He hath never been baited, for he is too childish and foolish and doth perform many tricks. Even Master Banks, he that hath the performing horse Morocco, was impressed.'

"'This Mummer bear looked not so gentle as he saved our life, thank God, did he not, Sir Robert?' said the Queen.

"'Tis true, he is a most wonderful bear Ma'am, I fed him with me own hand. Young Hamnet wishes him not to be baited.'"

"The Queen then demanded, 'And what is this bear's just reward to be?

Cecil leant forward and murmured in the Queen's ear.

The Queen then spoke again.

"Hamnet, your bear cub hath now grown exceeding large, I believe thy Father says, too large for home and too large to travel with the theatrical men. Would you wish him to stay in our Royal Menagerie in the Tower? I understand from Master Cecil that your father says that you are to return to Warwickshire, to Stratford-upon-Avon to school and then to Oxford to College.'

"And then I told the Queen that I would be sad to be parted from Mummer and not to see him. But she replied, 'Bear Mummer would be my guest and you can visit him. I have talked with thy father about this, and he hath said it would be a great kindness and that he would relieve somewhat the expense of the bear. This will ensure that Mummer lacks no comfort. Thy father is a true patriot, who knows that our Treasury is still sparse from the defence of the realm against the Armada.'

"Then she winked at Cecil. 'This Mummer Bear hath saved our life, hath he not, Sir Robert?' she asked again.

"'Tis true Ma'am,' answered Sir Robert, "and it is fit that he repose at the Tower. And Master Henslowe, the Master of the Queen's Bears, shall be at charges for his keep, with thy father too, so that the burden should not fall too hard on either man."

"So, Father, I led Mummer out of the Queen's presence, and here he is."

Master Shakespeare was speechless, dumb, and (strange for him!) lost for words. Then suddenly he patted my head and rubbed my neck most fondly and said, "Thanks be to God that no-one shot thee, Hamnet or thou brave Mummer!

Chapter 18
I reside at The Tower

And thus it was that I came to reside at the Tower of London in the great Menagerie there. Hamnet came with me, as did Ali, who was to be my carer. Indeed he soon became the Menagerie Assistant and helped the Chief Keeper to look after all the animals there. My quarters were a large gated yard; the gates were sealed up with metal bands but had a small door let into them. There was a small brick sleeping house and a pool which could be filled with water by pulling a chain – the water served both for my drinking and to bathe therein.

Master Henslowe and Master Shakespeare were to be charged for my keep and thus it was that I was mightily well fed. I was given a dozen hens' eggs and several bowls of porridge in the morning, some beefsteaks and much fruit and vegetables during the day and an evening meal, accompanied as a special treat with a small bucket of beer.

Hamnet said to me, "You shall repose here at the Tower for a while for your best safety and keeping. When the winter has passed and the summer sun shines again, I shall return from Stratford to be with thee again, sweet bear. Then we shall strut the stage once more as Mummer the Renowned Bear and his Master, Hamnet the Magnificent!

Then as dusk drew, Hamnet took his leave of me. Tears were in the eyes of both of us, and much sadness in our hearts. Had I known I was never to see my beloved Hamnet again, I would never have been able to let him go.

* **

There were few other creatures in the menagerie, because of the expense of keeping them and the Queen's frugality. Among them were two small white cubs, the strangest bears I had ever seen. They were in a cage next to mine at the Tower. These brother and sister bears spoke just a little bear language, but their version was the strangest I had ever heard, nor did they understand me very well, though I had spoken with Russian bears, Indian moon bears and bears from many a foreign land, both in captivity and free in the wild.

These little bears, Ag and Og, told me they came from a great frozen land of ice and wind and snow in the far north of the world, and that a Norse ship had found them floating upon an ice piece broken off the great icepack, after their mother had drowned. They had been sold when the ship, which belonged to traders, brought them to London, where all knew that the great sport of bear-baiting made bears prized creatures. Yet these two little cubs were a curiosity and the wily Mr Henslowe, having purchased them at the docks after being summoned thereto, had made a gift of them to the Queen. The Queen herself, being even wilier and a great deal meaner than Mr Henslowe, accepted the gift upon the condition that Mr Henslowe provided for their feed and sustenance. Thus we were all housed together, and soon our cages were opened so that we could go out daily and play in a small yard. Once a month our keepers took us, in chains, down to the moat around the Tower, wherein, upon ropes, we could swim.

I taught those little cubs as much as I knew – which was not very much at all I fear. I mentioned little of the baiting. I think they were to be kept as toys as I myself now seemed to have become.

*** *

So did I spend a winter in the Tower of London in the Great Menagerie. That winter did I hibernate in my stone hut. Having eaten most heartily through the autumn I had now become a very big bear indeed, but I was right royally treated and harmed in no way nor did I harm to any thing.

Chapter 19
I learn of Hamnet

Upon the first rays of spring sunshine, the Keeper took me down to the river, tied with a long chain secured by a strong rope to a stout stake driven into the riverbank next to the pier. I was allowed into the Thames, there to swim and fish. And most enjoyable it was to do so! Visitors would come and stand on the banks and battlements above us and watch my two keepers, Ali and a yeoman, as they managed out my rope. The weather changed and I knew by the lengthening of the days that summer was nearly upon us. I knew that Hamnet would soon visit me, at the start of the summer. Each day when the menagerie opened to visitors (who paid a penny) did I eagerly search for Hamnet but ne'er he came.

The summer was well nigh past when one day I found Judith and Master Shakespeare at my cage gates. I was at first right pleased to see them, as they came into my cage. I looked beyond them for the figure of Master Hamnet but saw him not. Judith came close to the cage and began to cry uncontrollably. I found myself crying too, although I knew not why. Some sense inside me told me that ill tidings had befallen Judith, so I hugged her.

Then Judith spoke, "My dear Mummer, your career in the Theatre has been cut short by the plague. My darling brother Hamnet hath died before his time. His life was indeed but a summer's lease. The plague hath taken your friend and rescuer, my wonderful brother from us – your performances with him can be no more."

I understood her words and mood only too well. I burst into a roaring weeping rage and ran around my caged yard, as fearful and unhappy as I had ever been. A blackness filled my soul and I wept – my tears for my lost mother were mingled with those I wept for Hamnet in my utter misery.

After some time, I held Judith tightly still. I felt from her something of Hamnet's lost love. I looked around at the menagerie, the yeomen moving about, the zebra, the camel, my neighboring white bear cubs, an insect that flew past me. They all had life, but Hamnet had he none.

Judith remembered her father's words as he looked on the lifeless body of his beautiful son: "Why should a horse, a dog, a rat, have life, and thou no breath at all?" Judith later told me that the last words Hamnet spake to his father Will were that he should take care of Mummer, that I never should be baited. Thus upon Hamnet's deathbed did his father the great showman and playwright thus solemnly swear.

** * * *

In his later years Master William Shakespeare, by then a great and noted playwright, would often visit the Tower and go up unto the menagerie therein, where he would give the Keepers a small purse with gold coins. He would come and sit in the bears' enclosure and talk to me while we ate strawberries which he had brought from Lambeth, near the Archbishop's palace. He would say, "Mummer, I remember when Hamnet brought those pedlar children back to our home where Mistress Anne fed them bread, apple juice, honey and egg. It was those children that found you Mummer," said Master William, a tear in his eye. "It was with them and their father that Hamnet bargained for you, with the Turkish golden piece with a hollow centre on a leather that I gave to him for his fifth birthday. Alas, so many years ago and Hamnet no longer with us!"

Chapter 20
Scotland

One day, Master William came unto me with Judith and Suzanne all fresh from Stratford. Suzanne held me tight and I held her close as we hugged in my cage. Suzanne said to me, "You are to retire to Scotland, Mummer. You will reside in peace upon a great private estate and will be well cared for."

Master William then spoke, "The Earl of Arklay remembers, when he was younger, seeing thee and Hamnet performing a comic show at the Rose. And he has invited you to reside at his home in the Highlands, in his great estate with its hills and forests."

Thus did I travel on a barge and then a sailing boat around the coast of Britain, together with a cargo of silks and fine pottery. Once aboard the sailing boat, I was allowed on deck with Tham and Ali; I was bound by a chain to the cage, but the air felt good and I am sure I could smell fish! I think that I supped of finer fare than the crew since Ali had brought with him sacks of oats, fruits, and the like.

They were afraid of me, those sailors, but Ali and Tham Greenaway travelled with me. Perchance there was some affair of state between Master William and the Earls, now that we had a new Scottish king. My travelling cage had been cleaned and much work had been done by locksmiths' men. I saw that below my quarters Tham and Mr Will had placed a heavy chest. So thus I sailed to Scotland still keeper of the Crown's treasures!

The wind was fresh and the boat had a smooth motion to it. We sailed along the coast of what had been Queen Elizabeth's England to her eternal neighbour, Scotland. The weather was warm and I arrived in Scotland in a small port. At the dock, Tham Greenaway had gone to organise the carriage and Ali stayed with me.

Then there was a journey by wagon, up into the Highlands of Scotland, past mountains and great open skies. Through forests and woodlands did I travel with Tham and Ali and a cart driver, through wide green plains, then more forests and, in the distance, some snow capped mountain peaks.

Soon we came to two great open gates, with winged birds atop each pillar – something that reminded me of Stander's description of the estate at which he had been held in Russia! The gates were rusty but had a glint of ancient golden paint. At the end of a long drive stood a great and ancient building, part house and part turreted castle.

For two nights I slept at the back of the great house in a shelter of straw which was a horse's stable, but on the third night I walked out in the moonlight, for I was no longer chained. I ambled further and slowly I climbed up the hill toward the great forest. I turned and looked back down at the house and there stood Ali watching me from a distance. I thought of Hamnet then and the sadness in my heart grew.

As I went on, I became hungry, so I foraged as I climbed awkwardly through the bracken bush and bark. I sniffed and then feasted upon stiff small apples and many berries from the trees and branches. There were berries everywhere and soon I was quite full up. Then I ventured higher and discovered among the rocks a fresh strong bubbling stream with fish leaping upwards. The smell of the fish was strong and there were many of them splashing up the waterfall.

Then suddenly I could smell bear! Not just any bear – it was Stander! And that was his laugh that I heard! I was free and with my old friend. No more of London's heat, full of the smells of men; no more fear of the bear-baiting – but to be free in the forest, the place where bears were meant to be, and with a brave bear who knew all there was to know about living in the wild. This was the life for me!

Printed in Great Britain
by Amazon

41523680R00059